MW01287158

Books for Girls

4 Great Stories
For 8 to 12 year olds

Katrina Kahler, B Campbell, Kaz Campbell

Table of Contents

Julia Jones' Diary Book 1 - My Worst Day Ever!

This is how it all started...

The last thing I remember is the look of horror on the faces of the audience. But what had caused me to feel the most humiliation was when I noticed Blake Jansen, the coolest boy in our class, staring down at me in disbelief.

My memory of that night still fills me with shame. Everyone says that I was lucky to get away with only a mild concussion and a huge lump on my head. But the disgrace I had felt at being the laughing stock of the whole school was still very fresh in my mind.

I'd really like to try and forget that entire day, erase it from my memory banks forever, but right now it keeps coming back to haunt me. Loser with a capital L! That's the way I feel about myself right now. I still can't believe the events of that fateful day. If only it were a nightmare I could wake up from and never ever have to think about again. But unfortunately, that is just not the case!

Mom says that time heals all wounds and that everyone else has probably completely forgotten the incident, but I think it's going to take quite a while for me to get over it. For some reason though, I suspect that one particular girl in our class had something to do with it all. Call it gut instinct or intuition, but I have a sneaking suspicion that somehow she was involved.

Thinking back before that doomed day, life had been pretty good. My best friend, Millie and I had auditioned for the school musical and we were both selected for major roles. Being in grade seven gave us an advantage over the younger kids, that and of course the fact that we were both dancers.

The best part was that we'd also been asked to choreograph sections of the performance and this was a huge honor.

Miss Sheldon, the performing arts teacher who was in charge of the production, had given us the responsibility of coming up with some routines and teaching the other kids the dance moves they needed to learn. We were so excited about this, especially because we'd been left in charge. Miss Sheldon is the coolest teacher ever!

There are some great dancers in our grade; even some of the boys are particularly good. One boy named Alex has been dancing pretty much his entire life and is probably the best dancer in the whole school. When he was younger, he said that the other kids had bullied him and called him a girl as well as a heap of horrible names that he really didn't want to mention. But I could see that everyone had finally developed a huge amount of respect for Alex and those who were still unaware of his talents were in for a big surprise. Hip hop is his specialty and he's so cool to watch. I kept telling him that when he's old enough, he should audition for 'So You Think You Can Dance,' and he told me that he'd really like to.

As well as Alex, there's another kid in our grade who is kind of overweight and dorky looking. But it turns out that he has an awesome voice.

I had no idea that our school has so much talent and it certainly came as a huge surprise to find out that Liam can actually sing really well. The look of amazement when we heard his audition pretty much spread like wild fire. I even caught the teachers raising their eyebrows in astonishment.

It just goes to show you that you can't judge a book by its cover! I never really understood what that meant until hearing Liam sing. Now, I don't think I'll ever look at him in the same way again. It's also a really big lesson for me. From now on, I will never judge a person by their looks alone. I'll wait till I get to know them because I've found out that until you do get to know people, you really don't know what type of person they are or what hidden talents they might have.

Anyway, the musical was shaping up to be a huge success. The dance troupe we had put together was really coming along and we rehearsed during every lunch break and sometimes even after school. Then one afternoon, an amazing thing happened; Blake Jansen, who I've had a secret crush on since the fourth grade, turned up at rehearsals with his friend, Jack.

At first I was embarrassed to see them watching us and to make matters worse, some of the girls actually starting to giggle and carry on. One girl was even fluttering her eyelashes! I'd heard about that sort of thing but had never seen it in action before. Talk about humiliating! I just tried to ignore the boys at first but after about ten minutes of observing our routine, they walked towards Millie and I and actually asked if they could join in.

I couldn't believe it! Blake Jansen really wanted to join our dance troupe! I was sure it was because Alex was involved and everyone was starting to hear how cool he was. But I didn't care about the reason. Having a couple more boys included would just make it so much better! Although, I was reluctant to admit to myself that I was particularly glad one of the boys just happened to be Blake.

Blake

Millie grinned at me and whispered quietly, "Julia…can you believe Blake is joining us!" I pretended I didn't hear her and went into a spiel telling the boys that if they wanted to be involved, they'd have to commit to rehearsals and put in one hundred per cent effort.

Much to my surprise, they were really enthusiastic about the whole thing and couldn't wait to get started. I thought it was awesome they were keen to take part. And surprisingly enough, they turned out to be pretty good. It was shaping up to be a highlight of the musical and I began to really look forward to every rehearsal. Of course having Blake there helped to keep my enthusiasm levels high but I just had to make sure I didn't give him too much attention. I didn't want him thinking that I actually liked him. That would just be too embarrassing!

But, apart from Blake Jansen and constant rehearsals, I really had no idea what was ahead for us. If I had only known at the time, I probably would never have volunteered to take part in the musical at all.

The new girl...

The weeks passed by and school went on as usual. However, as the final performance day drew closer, our practice sessions became more frequent and we were kept very busy.

Millie and I had been asked to choreograph the dance routines for several additional scenes as well, so we had little time for anything else.

Then one morning, just as the bell was ringing and everyone was heading into class, a very pretty girl with blonde wavy hair who looked to be about our age, happened to arrive at our classroom door.

"Come in, Sara!" I heard Mrs. Jackson call out in a friendly manner. "I've been expecting you!"

Everyone looked curiously in the girl's direction. "Girls and boys, I'd like you to meet Sara Hamilton. She has just enrolled at our school and will now be joining our class."

Sara smiled shyly as she followed Mrs. Jackson towards an empty desk next to mine.

"Julia, I'm sure you'll be happy to look after Sara and show her around the school during break times today. Please make her welcome."

"Yes of course, Mrs. Jackson," I answered with enthusiasm as I smiled encouragingly towards Sara. "Hi, Sara! My name's Julia and this is my friend, Millie," I added, pointing towards Millie who was seated on the other side of me.

Millie smiled brightly and jumped up to help Sara unpack her bag and put her books and other belongings into her desk drawer. It was an unusual event to have a new student come to our school and when it happened it was always very exciting. I could see all the other kids in the class looking towards Sara with interest and by the time the bell rang for morning break, Sara was surrounded by girls who were desperately keen to meet her.

We all headed down the stairs towards the area where the grade seven kids sat to eat their morning tea. There was a large group trying to get Sara's attention, so Millie and I sat back in order to avoid overwhelming the poor girl who was swamped with people asking her questions.

As I looked around, I realized that she also had the attention of pretty much every other kid in the grade, the boys included.

Sara was very pretty and was wearing the coolest clothes. I noticed her white sandals; they had straps around the ankles and chunky heels, the latest in fashion and very expensive.

I also realized that she was wearing the pleated suede skirt I had been eyeing off in the window of a local designer store on the weekend. Judging by the reaction of all the girls, I could tell that she was going to be very popular and I wondered suddenly if she was good at dancing.

When the opportunity arose, Millie and I moved closer to Sara and began chatting. She was super friendly and seemed really nice. We found out that she and her family had just moved into town the week before, as her dad had been transferred to a new job in the area.

Sara told us how much she had been looking forward to starting at a new school. She didn't say too much but I kind of got the feeling that the kids at her last school weren't very nice to her. I reassured her that she wouldn't have that problem at our school as all the girls in our class got on really well.

"I've noticed that there are some cute boys here as well," she said to Millie and I with a huge grin.

We grinned back and Millie said, "Yeah, some of them are ok!" with a wink in my direction. I could see that Sara was watching my reaction to Millie's comment and I couldn't help but blush. Trying to change the subject I asked Sara, "Do you like dancing?"

"Oh, I love dancing!" she exclaimed. "It's my favorite thing to do. I was taking hip hop classes before I left my old school and I'm really keen to start up again."

"Oh wow!" I replied. "If you're good at hip hop, you could probably join in our hip hop dance for the musical. It's in four weeks, so you'd have time to learn the routine. Do you want to come to rehearsals at lunch time?"

"I'd love to!" Sara answered. "Thank you so much for inviting me."

"That's alright," I beamed in response. "I'll just have to check with Miss Sheldon but I'm sure it will be fine. She's keen to have as many kids involved as possible."

Chatting excitedly, we headed back to class, explaining what the musical was about and the different dances that Millie and I had choreographed. "It's going to be the most awesome thing ever!" Millie gasped. "The costumes are amazing and we can hardly wait for the night to come."

"This is really cool!" Sara grinned excitedly. "I had a feeling about this school. I knew that it was going to be the right place for me."

As we walked up the stairs, I felt a shiver of excitement run down my spine. "What an unexpected surprise," I thought to myself. I certainly hadn't expected to be making a cool new friend when I arrived at school that morning.

And with beaming smiles, the three of us headed towards our desks and sat down to get on with the work that Mrs. Jackson had put on the board.

Feeling a bit jealous...

It turned out that Sara was very good at hip hop. Actually, she was not just good, she was pretty incredible. The moves that she knew how to do were some that I had never seen before and she was extremely flexible as well. I looked on in amazement while she demonstrated a routine that she'd been working on before she left her old school.

As I glanced around our group, I noticed that everyone else was also looking on in awe. It was hard not to. Her blonde pigtails swung from side to side as she flipped and turned. And the cargo green outfit that she wore was so cool, a perfect hip hop style that matched her clear complexion and blonde hair beautifully.

I glanced down at my shabby shorts that I had quickly changed into before rehearsal and for the first time felt aware of how uncool they were. Usually I didn't worry too much about things like that, especially just for a rehearsal. But having Sara in our midst, looking so perfect, really made me think twice about the way I was dressed.

When she finished, everyone congratulated her and told her how amazing she was. She certainly deserved it and I thought about how lucky we were to have her join us. By incorporating some of the moves that she knew, our dance was sure to be a stand out performance.

We decided to get Sara to demonstrate and everyone was concentrating quite intensely as some of the interchanges were very tricky. Then just when I thought everyone had got the hang of it, Sara stepped over next to Blake and grabbed his arms to show him how he should be moving them.

"It's more this type of action, Blake!" she explained to him as he looked at her with those big brown eyes of his, following her demonstration closely.

"You've almost got it, you just need to make your movements more abrupt and deliberate," she continued.

And when he suddenly mimicked her movements to perfection her squeal was full of obvious delight. "That's it!" she cried. "That's perfect!"

Sara

And with a proud grin, Blake replied, "Thanks heaps, Sara! Thanks for your help." Then obviously very pleased with himself, he continued with the remainder of the routine before joining in with the rest of us to put the new version of our dance together.

"That's such a cool dance, Sara!" Alex exclaimed when we had finally finished. "It's awesome to have a girl who's so good at hip hop at our school."

"Yeah, that was great, Sara," Jack chimed in, obviously not wanting to miss out on getting her attention.

"Thanks!" Sara replied in a modest manner. "You guys are really good dancers too!"

As I packed up my gear and headed on over towards them, I couldn't help but notice the smile on Blake's face as he chatted easily with Sara. They looked like they were getting on really well. And as I watched her talking happily with the group of boys, I guessed that Sara would probably get along with just about everyone.

Something feels wrong...

"Oh my gosh!" Millie exclaimed. "Look who's sitting down at a table in McDonald's right now!"

I followed the direction of Millie's gaze where to my surprise, I spotted Blake, Jack and Alex, the three boys from our dance troupe at school. Their undivided attention was cast towards a girl whose back was towards us. But I knew that I would recognize that flowing long, blonde hair anywhere.

"What are they all doing here together?" asked Millie, curiously.

"I have no idea!" I replied, "But let's go find out." And I strode quickly over towards their table.

Millie and I had decided to spend Saturday afternoon at the mall. I'd had my eye on a really pretty top that had recently come into stock in my favorite store and I had decided I would use my birthday money to buy it. However, to my huge dismay, on entering the store a few minutes earlier, I had discovered that there were none left in my size.

When Millie realized how hugely disappointed I was, she offered to buy me a thick shake at McDonalds to try and cheer me up. That was when we happened to notice our friends from school.

"Hey guys," I said in a friendly manner. "What are you all doing here?"

They had been so absorbed in Sara's conversation, that they had not seen us approach and got quite a start at the unexpected sound of my voice.

"Julia!" Sara exclaimed, "And Millie! What a surprise to see you here." They all shuffled over to make room at the booth for us and although the boys welcomed us without hesitation, I kind of got the impression that Sara did not feel the same way. An uncomfortable tension seemed to appear out of nowhere but then I decided I must be imagining things. So I started chatting aimlessly about it being such a coincidence to run into each other like that. The boys explained that they had been to see a movie and had then bumped into Sara afterwards, just as they were entering McDonalds.

"I was shopping with my mom," Sara said. "When I saw the boys, Mom told me I could meet up with her in about half an hour so I could have some time to hang out with them."

Grinning in Blake's direction she continued, "The boys said they might even come to my house tomorrow so we can do some extra rehearsals. You girls can come as well if you want, but if you're too busy, then that's ok. We can just practice at school on Monday."

"I can't make it tomorrow," replied Millie, obviously disappointed. "We're going to visit my grandparents so I'll be out for the whole day."

"Oh, that's too bad!" answered Sara. "Never mind, we can all get together on Monday."

"Julia can probably go, though," Millie quickly responded. "You were saying earlier that you had nothing to do tomorrow, Julia!"

Looking towards Sara, I replied, "Only if that's ok with you, Sara."

"Oh, that's fine, Julia. Of course you can come. I'm planning on teaching the boys some other dance moves that I know.

So I can teach you too, if you like."

"That sounds great," I answered, trying to muster some enthusiasm. For some reason though, I didn't feel completely welcome and sat there quietly while Sara continued her animated conversation; with the boys as her main audience.

I suddenly noticed a familiar looking carry bag sitting on the seat between myself and Sara and then recognized it as coming from my favorite clothing store.

"Have you been shopping at Dream Warehouse?" I asked Sara curiously. "That's my favorite store."

"Yes," Sara replied brightly. "I just bought the prettiest top, only about fifteen minutes ago. As soon as I saw it, I just had to have it and I'm so lucky because it was the last one in my size! Do you like it?" she asked, pulling it out of the bag.

I gasped in surprise when I realized that it was the exact same top that I had intended to buy for myself and when I looked at it more closely, I spotted the label and realized that it was also in my size. Sara had beaten me to it. "What are the chances of that?" I sighed to myself as I commented on how pretty it was.

I decided not to mention that I had actually planned on buying that very top, but then out of the blue, Millie exclaimed, "Sara, that looks like the top you wanted to buy. Isn't it exactly the same one? And it's in your size as well!"

Seeing my expression, Sara responded, "Oh Julia, did I beat you to it? I'm so sorry!"

For some reason, I felt that she really wasn't being sincere, but I told her not to worry about it and decided to put it out of my mind. I didn't know what was bugging me. "Perhaps

I'm coming down with something?" I wondered. "Or maybe I'm just being silly. Sara is a really nice girl, it's obvious how much everyone likes her and we're really lucky to have her in our class."

As Millie and I sat on the bus heading home later that afternoon, I decided to push all the crazy thoughts about Sara from my mind. We really were fortunate to have her come to our school and to actually have her talent included in our dance troupe was something to be very grateful for.

I decided to focus on attempting some new hip hop moves myself that I could share with the guys the next day and tried to remove all the uneasy thoughts from my mind. But for some reason, I just couldn't shake the foreboding premonition that seemed to be tingling down my spine.

Envy...

As I lay in bed on Sunday night, thinking about the afternoon that I had spent at Sara's house, the previous thoughts that I'd been having on my way home from the mall the day before, were furthest from my mind.

It turned out that the boys couldn't make it as some other stuff had apparently come up, but in the end I was glad. It was so nice to spend time alone with Sara and I found that when it was just the two of us, we got along really well.

She lives in the coolest house. It's really big and super modern. They even have a spa bath in the bathroom as well as a jacuzzi out by the pool. We talked about spending time sunbathing in her backyard as soon as the weather was warm enough. The lounge chairs that were scattered around the sides of the pool were so inviting that I had to try them out. Then when I found that they reclined right back, I laid there picturing myself during the summer months, just relaxing by that beautiful sparkling pool.

Sara is so lucky! She seems to have pretty much everything a girl could wish for. Her bedroom has the prettiest pink wallpaper with a gorgeous white flower print as a feature wall. And her furniture is all white. She has a huge comfy bed with matching bedside tables. I've never known a girl our age to have a queen sized bed though. Even my parents only have a double bed and Sara's bed seems enormous in comparison.

The two hot pink chrome lamps that sit on her bedside tables are the coolest design and I just love the fluffy pink rug that spreads across the middle of her floor. And she even has a window seat that looks out through a big white framed window, across the landscaped back yard and pool area. I've always dreamed of having a window seat like that, it's just like in the movies.

It's pretty difficult not to feel just a little bit jealous of Sara though. She has so much cool stuff and she is so pretty. But I guess being an only child is the reason why her parents spoil her so much. It would probably be hard not to spoil an only child. I only met her mom briefly but she seems very nice. Although, Sara said that her parents are rarely at home and I was actually lucky to meet her mother. Apparently her dad's office is in town but he has to travel a lot and her mom is always out doing something or other, Sara isn't really sure what.

I thought that was pretty strange; not really knowing what your mom does every day and hardly seeing your parents. Sara said that it's good not having parents to annoy her because she can do whatever she wants when they're not around. It's a bit of a weird situation, but I guess everyone is different.

They're certainly very different to my family, that's for sure. There's no way I'd be allowed to have all that freedom! My parents want to know what I'm up to all the time. They check on where I am and what time I will be home and who I am spending time with. And we always eat meals together, breakfast and dinner anyway; as well as that, we have regular family time where we play board games or watch a movie or go on an outing together somewhere.

My brother, Matt is getting sick of family time and often complains because he would rather be hanging out with his friends. I guess boys his age are like that, but I still like being around my family.

I rolled over and stared out the window and into the night sky. There was a full moon shining and its light was beaming into my room, making it hard for me to go to sleep. I didn't want to close the curtain though, as I love watching the stars at night time, especially from the comfort of my bed.

As I finally started to drift off, visions of Sara came to mind. She was dressed in the most incredible hip hop outfit and was bowing to applause from an adoring audience, her wide smile beaming across her face. I pictured myself sitting amongst the crowd and cheering her on as well.

Then abruptly, I sat up with a start. A cold shiver had run right through me and I could feel the hairs on my arms standing on end. Unsure of what had caused the sudden disturbing feeling, I looked around my room and realized the window was wide open so I jumped up to close it. Hopping back into bed, I rolled over and closed my eyes. We had an early rehearsal planned in the morning before school so I needed to get up early. I pulled the covers up to my chin and fell into a deep sleep.

The take-over begins...

Our early morning rehearsal didn't turn out quite as I had expected.

When I arrived at the prearranged time, I was very surprised to see Sara and the rest of the gang already there and by the look of their sweat drenched faces, it appeared that they'd been practicing for quite some time already.

"Where have you been?" Alex asked. "Did you miss the bus or something?"

Looking confused, I checked the time on my watch. "I thought we'd arranged to start at eight am," I replied. "And that's still five minutes away."

"Hey guys!" called Millie as she approached from behind me. "Have you already started?"

I looked from Millie to Alex to Sara and then to the rest of the group, shaking my head in confusion. I could see that Blake had a weird look on his face but then Sara's voice broke the silence.

"Oh, Julia!" she exclaimed. "I called Blake last night and we decided to get an early start. I thought that someone would have contacted you girls to let you know."

Blake frowned and looked in Sara's direction, obviously confused about what she was saying. But without missing a beat, she continued, "Well, never mind! You're here now, so why don't you just join in? We've made a few changes to the routine. I hope you like it. Everyone else thinks it's really cool!"

Glancing towards Millie who was shrugging her shoulders as if to indicate that she had no idea what was going on, we stood back and watched as everyone demonstrated what they'd been working on.

"The guys are keen for me to be in the lead at the front," Sara explained, while trying to catch her breath after they'd finished what I had to admit was a very impressive routine.

I looked around at the group and they all seemed to be looking in any direction except towards me. So I replied in a quiet voice, "Well, if that's what everyone wants, then I guess that's how we'll do the dance."

Trying to muster some enthusiasm, I joined Millie in the second row to rehearse the new moves a few more times. All the while, my head was spinning.

"I know I'm not in charge," I thought frantically to myself, "And everyone should certainly have a say in what we do. But I'm really not sure what's going on here!"

"Ok!" called Sara brightly, about ten minutes later as she suddenly called the rehearsal to a close. "That was great guys. This new routine is really coming together. Let's meet up again early tomorrow morning. Julia and Millie, do you think you can make it? If we all arrive by seven-thirty, we'll have plenty of time for a good rehearsal!"

And without even waiting for an answer, she strode off towards the locker room, to have a quick shower before heading to class.

"What just happened?" Millie whispered, a frown of misunderstanding still very evident on her face.

"I have no idea!" I replied and then followed her into the locker room so we could also get showered and changed before the bell went.

Walking slowly back to class, I watched Sara striding alongside Blake, just ahead of Millie and I, chatting away in her usual animated manner. Then when we sat down at our desks, she smiled towards me as if nothing unusual whatsoever had happened. I looked at Mrs. Jackson who had begun explaining a new Math concept but found it very difficult to concentrate. Visions of the morning's rehearsal were floating around in my head and I could not get Sara's confident voice out of my mind.

"Julia!" Mrs. Jackson repeated for the second time. "Are you listening or not?"

"I have just said your name three times and you still aren't answering my question. Would you rather do this work during break time?"

"Sorry, Mrs. Jackson!" I replied in a worried tone, "Is the answer twenty-two?"

"Oh my goodness, Julia!" she explained. "You haven't been listening to a word I've said. I think you'd better stay behind and complete this activity during morning tea break. Maybe then you'll decide to concentrate!"

Glancing towards Millie, I felt grateful for her genuine look of sympathy but the grin that remained on Sara's face was not something I had expected to see and a worried knot started to form in the pit of my stomach.

Am I being paranoid?...

Sitting at the dinner table that night, I didn't feel very hungry at all. I sat there picking at my food, while my brother, Matt went on and on about the goal he had scored at footy training that afternoon.

As if I was interested in his football game! I really don't like football at all and was so glad that I didn't have to suffer being dragged along to his training sessions and games anymore. Finally, I'm old enough to stay at home on my own, rather than facing boredom at the football field every weekend.

My parents however, both love football, especially my dad and they took great interest in Matt's conversation about the season and how well his team were doing in the competition. In a way though, I was glad they had something to occupy them which took their attention away from me as I really didn't feel like talking about the day I'd had.

Morning tea break had consisted of me having to sit at my desk eating the food from my lunchbox, while doing extra Math. That was my punishment for not listening during the morning's lesson.

Then when I was finally allowed to go out, Millie and I had to attend a meeting for the committee in charge of the musical. We were asked to report on the progress of the dances we'd been choreographing and practicing. Then we were informed of a dress rehearsal which was scheduled to take place in two weeks' time and were given information to distribute to everyone.

So overall, it hadn't been the best of days. Although Sara had maintained her friendly manner and continued as if everything were normal, I wasn't so sure. Well, in the scheme of things, I guess everything was ok and I wondered if it were all in my imagination. Was I just being jealous and immature? And was I being a total control freak? Even though I had organized the dances and the choreography, along with Millie's help, it didn't mean that I had to be in charge of our group's dance.

Sara is an exceptional dancer, and I really have to admit that she is very talented. I should be grateful for her support and the way in which our routine has improved since she joined us. But I just couldn't shake the uneasy feeling that I had been overcome with since arriving at rehearsal that morning.

With a dejected sigh, I excused myself from the table under the pretext that I had homework to complete. Luckily my mom was still so absorbed in Matt's excited ramblings that she neglected to remind me it was my turn to do the dishes.

I headed up to my room and tried to concentrate on the homework that was due the following day. More Math! That was certainly not what I felt like doing, but rather than having to face the wrath of my teacher the following morning, I forced myself to concentrate so I could just get it over with.

When I turned out the light a couple of hours later and hopped into bed, I decided that the next day I would join in with everyone else and focus on a good rehearsal. "I'm not going to let Sara bother me," I thought to myself as I closed my eyes. "I'll just be my usual friendly self and I'm sure that everything will be fine!"

We had the school musical to look forward to and it was the highlight of the year so far. I was determined that nothing was going to spoil it!

She's like a Super Hero...

An unexpected surprise awaited us when we entered the school grounds the next morning. Millie and I had caught the same bus and as we were determined to be on time for rehearsal, we raced off the bus and through the school gates in an excited rush.

In the school car park however, where there would normally only be a few cars belonging to teachers at that time of the morning, we discovered several vans parked haphazardly and a large crowd of students milling around trying to find out what was going on.

Pushing through the crowd, curious to find out what had grasped everyone's attention, we spotted two policemen questioning our school principal, Mr. Davis.

Then immediately behind him were a couple of men with large microphones and some sophisticated looking camera equipment. They appeared to be from the local TV station and were interviewing a group of kids. When I managed to get closer, I realized that right in the middle of the group with the microphone pointed directly towards her, was Sara Hamilton.

"It was so scary!" Sara was saying. "But as soon as I heard the smash, I ran to the office to get help."

"You are a very quick thinking young lady!" the reporter acknowledged Sara with a look of admiration.

"Well, I just did what I thought I should," Sara explained. "When I saw the smoke coming from the broken window, I knew that something was terribly wrong!"

"If Sara hadn't acted as quickly as she had, the whole building could have burnt down!" exclaimed Miss Fitz, the drama teacher who was standing beside her.

"You're very lucky to have such a responsible young lady attending your school!" the reporter who was conducting the interview commented enthusiastically.

Sara, how does it feel to be a hero?

"Yes, we are very proud of Sara, she is new to our school and as you say, we are very lucky to have her here as a student!" chimed in Mr. Davis, beaming with pride in Sara's direction.

The reporters asked Mr. Davis a few more questions and ended the interview. Sara was then quickly surrounded by a surge of kids trying to get close to her in order to be captured on camera. By that time, more kids had arrived for school and the car park was ablaze with excitement. It was not every day that a television camera crew along with several members of the police force turned up, and everyone was keen to get in on the action.

Mr. Dawson, the physical education teacher blew his whistle and told everyone to go to class or wherever they should be at that time of the morning. Then it wasn't until we reached our classroom that Millie and I could actually find out the exact details of what had happened.

Mrs. Jackson explained to us all that Sara had been at school early, in preparation for our dance rehearsal. Apparently as she had walked across the car park, towards the Performing Arts hall, she'd heard a loud smash of glass. When she went around to the rear of the building to investigate, she noticed smoke and flames billowing from the window.

She had then rushed for help and very luckily, had bumped into the janitor who happened to be cleaning the area around the office, which was still fairly deserted at that time of the morning. He and Sara raced back to the building where they'd spotted a couple of teenage boys running from the scene. Between the two of them, Sara and the janitor had managed to get a nearby garden hose connected so they could put out the fire.

Without their quick thinking, the building could have burnt down and that would have been the end of the musical, as it was the only building that was suitable for the performance.

Just as Mrs. Jackson finished sharing the main details, Sara walked into the classroom. Everyone stared in her direction and then a loud burst of applause and cheering erupted. "Three cheers for Sara!" someone at the back of the room called out.

"Hip, Hip, Hooray! Hip, Hip, Hooray! Hip, Hip, Hooray!" the applause was deafening and Sara sat down at her desk, beaming proudly while kids rushed to pat her on the back and give her high fives.

I spotted Blake looking at her with open admiration. She

really was a hero and deserved all the accolades she was getting. It would have been disastrous if the building had burnt down. It could even have led to the whole school going up in flames.

As everyone returned to their desks, I congratulated her warmly. She was the most popular girl in the school at that moment and I could see that everyone wanted to be her friend.

When Mrs. Jackson directed us to take out our Math books so we could begin work, I caught Sara smiling happily in Blake's direction. He was grinning widely across the room towards her as well and it was obvious that they had certainly become close. I looked at Millie who had also noticed the exchange and she raised her eyebrows questioningly.

Sara glanced at me with a smug kind of grin, maintaining intense eye contact for a few seconds and then quickly refocused her attention on her math book.

"Pay attention please, Julia! It's time to get on with our lessons now." I heeded Mrs. Jackson's warning and looked towards the board.

It was full of Math equations but once again, I struggled to concentrate. I really wasn't sure whether I had a real friend in Sara or not and began to suspect that she may not be the girl she had so far portrayed herself to be. I then wondered what agenda she had in mind.

As I sat there, I considered the questions racing through my mind. Did I just have an over active imagination or were my instincts picking up on something that was not as it seemed? I guessed that only time would tell!

The birthday party…

Finally it was the weekend. I jumped out of bed early on Saturday morning eager to have breakfast and be ready when Millie arrived to pick me up.

Our week had been very hectic! Since the incident in the Performing Arts building, we were forced to do our rehearsals in a small adjoining room while the damage to the main area was being repaired. And unfortunately, it wasn't free very often so we had to make the most of the limited amount of time that we were given to use it.

Sara's hero status had escalated and as I had predicted, everyone wanted to be her friend. Although I sat next to her in class and she was always polite and reasonably friendly, it seemed that she didn't have time for Millie and I during breaks anymore. She was too preoccupied with all the new friends she had made, including of course, Blake Jansen.

Meanwhile, Millie and I continued to work with the other dance groups and the younger kids whose dances we had to coordinate and choreograph, which kept us pretty busy ourselves.

But now that Saturday had finally arrived, I looked forward with enthusiasm to the day ahead. After a couple of days of heavy rain, the sun was shining and it promised to be a beautiful day. Jackie, one of the girls in our class had invited a group of friends to her house to celebrate her birthday. She lived on a large property that was situated on the outskirts of town. Most of us lived in the suburbs and never got the chance to do all the fun things that are possible when you own lots of land, so we were all really excited about it.

I had been there once for her birthday party years before and I remembered vividly, the amazing day I had experienced. One of the highlights had been a trailer ride that her dad had taken us all on. He had hooked up their open box trailer to the back of his four wheel drive and everyone had climbed into the back. Even two of our teachers had hopped in with us.

I remembered thinking how lucky Jackie was to have our teachers at her birthday party but now that idea seems pretty ridiculous. Having our current teacher, Mrs. Jackson at a birthday party is not something I could imagine anyone in my class wanting to arrange. It would be different if she were young and cool like Miss Fitz, our drama teacher, but Mrs. Jackson is pretty old now and I don't think that she'd enjoy it either!

There were about twenty kids at the time as well as the teachers, all squashed into the back of that trailer. Although I guess because the kids were quite small, we managed to fit in reasonably well. Everyone had been screaming and cheering as Jackie's dad drove around and around this huge grassy area and up their dirt driveway then back down again. The excitement we felt when he went over bumps on the road or the grass was so intense that none of us had wanted him to stop.

That trailer ride really was a highlight of my childhood and back then, I thought that Jackie was the luckiest kid alive to grow up on a property like that. And reminiscing about that day made me wonder if they still had that trailer because I thought it would still be a pretty cool thing to do!

When I jumped into the back of Millie's car later that morning, I was filled with excited anticipation about what lay ahead. Blake, Jack and Alex had also been invited and it was pretty much all that everyone had been able to talk about at school the day before. Sitting alongside Millie, we chatted about how much fun the party was going to be as well as how we were looking forward to giving Jackie her birthday present. We had gone shopping at the mall after school one day earlier in the week and were so happy with what we had bought.

The light blue jacket studded with silver sequins and a cool design on the collar and cuffs of the sleeves had definitely stood out on the rack. And because we'd had enough money left over from what we had pooled together, we were also able to buy her a really pretty silver necklace with a capital J on it. She had always admired the one I wore, which my mom had given me for my last birthday. It was just very lucky that we had gone shopping when the sales were on as the prices for everything were drastically reduced. That meant we were able to get her an extra special present and we couldn't wait to give it to her!

When we jumped out of the car, we saw Jackie running towards us, a huge grin on her face. We were the first to arrive and she was bubbling over with excitement.

We gave her a hug and handed her the present that we had carefully wrapped in shimmering pink paper, along with a darker shade of curling ribbon tied decoratively around it.

She could see our impatience in wanting her to open it straight away but decided to place it on a table on the veranda of her house so that all the presents could be opened later on, when everyone was there together.

While we were waiting for the others, she showed us around her property. Since my last visit, her parents had made some incredible changes to the outside entertaining area of their home. Where there was once just a large patch of green grass, now sat a huge sparkling swimming pool to which was attached an amazing looking diving deck at one end. Although summer had not yet arrived, the temperature that day was unusually warm. In addition, her parents had activated the pool's heating system in preparation for the party so the water would also be a lovely temperature.

There were streamers and balloons strung everywhere including on the walls and framework of a nearby gazebo and this really added to the birthday party atmosphere.

While we waited for the others to arrive, Jackie offered to take us over to the horse paddocks. As well as all the other advantages of living on a property, Jackie also had a pony of her own. He was a beautiful chestnut welsh mountain pony called Charlie and was the cutest thing I had ever seen.

Ever since I was a little girl, I had always dreamed of owning my own pony one day and I gently stroked his forehead, wistfully thinking about how much I would love to have my own horse. He eagerly took the carrots from our hands that Jackie had given us to feed to him and his rough tongue tickled my skin as he licked up the last remnants of carrot that remained.

"You will have to come over more often," Jackie said to us, especially when she realized how taken with her pony we were.

"We'd love to!" Millie and I replied in unison.

"You have the coolest property, Jackie," I continued. "You're so lucky!!"

Jackie smiled in response and then said, "Come on, we'd better head back. The others may be here already!"

We raced towards the house just as several cars were pulling up in the driveway. It seemed that everyone was arriving at once. People were jumping out of cars and within minutes, Jackie was laden with gifts from all her guests. Then I noticed Sara strolling down the driveway with her mom. She had so many items that she needed help to carry it all. And in her hands was a huge box that was gift wrapped in the most beautiful lilac colored wrapping paper with an enormous white bow adorning the top.

"Oh my gosh, Sara!" Jackie exclaimed. "What is inside that parcel?"

"Oh, it's just something small!" Sara replied sweetly. "But I hope you like it!"

Right behind Sara, I saw Blake and his friend, Jack. When Sara spotted them both, I could see her sudden spark of interest.

"Hi boys!" she called out in her usual friendly manner. "Can you please help me with all of this?" And she indicated the gear that her mom was carrying for her. They quickly moved to relieve her of all the bags and bits and pieces and then followed Sara into the house.

Trailing Jackie into her bedroom, the girls all stored their belongings and quickly got changed to go swimming. Because the boys were already dressed in swimming trunks, they had raced straight down to the pool, keen to get into the water. In typical boy style, by the time the girls joined them the boys were already doing bomb dives off the trampoline that stood by the pool's edge.

Squealing with excitement at being splashed, the girls stood by laughing and giggling as they watched the boys in action.

"I'm going to try that too!" Sara exclaimed as she followed Blake up onto the trampoline.

"Only two are allowed on the trampoline at once," Jackie warned as Alex and a couple of the girls tried to climb up and join in the fun.

"But we can all jump off the diving deck together!" Jackie continued, running around to the other side of the pool and onto the large diving platform.

"This is an awesome setup, Jackie!" called out Sara as she gave Blake a shove into the pool and then bomb dived into the water right next to him.

I stood alongside Millie, watching everyone and in particular, Sara who was paying so much attention to Blake. It was clearly obvious that she really liked him and it seemed that she wanted him and everyone else to know it.

Grabbing his head, she tried to dunk him under the water but he quickly swam away, jumped out of the pool and back onto the trampoline.

"Show us your biggest bomb dive, Blake," Sara called out,

but he just grinned and kept bouncing on the tramp.

"Let's go in," Millie called, grabbing my hand and leading me onto the diving deck.

Holding hands, we ran and did a big jump into the pool together. I was determined to just enjoy myself and not worry about Sara or Blake.

It was shaping up to be a great party and there was too much fun to be had, to be bothered worrying about them.

Just then I noticed Becky, one of the girls from our dance group, sitting on a chair in the gazebo watching everyone in the water.

"Becky!" I called. "Aren't you coming in?" Becky hadn't changed into her swimmers and I wondered why.

Hopping out of the pool, I grabbed my towel and went over to join her. When I asked again why she wasn't swimming, she simply replied that she didn't want to.

By that time, Millie had joined us and quietly whispered in my ear. "She's too embarrassed to put swimmers on."

I looked at Becky with sympathy. She was such a nice girl but had developed a real paranoia about her weight. Even though she wasn't what you would call fat, she had become very self-conscious about her body and I remembered that towards the end of the previous summer she had started declining all offers to go swimming. No one else had commented, but Millie and I had figured out the reason why.

"It's so much fun, Becky and the water is really warm!" I coaxed. "Why don't you put your swimmers on and hop in with us?"

"I forgot to bring them," she explained in a quiet voice.

I knew that she would intentionally have left them behind, but then I suggested that she could borrow a pair from Jackie.

"Oh no, that's ok," she replied. "They probably wouldn't fit me anyway! I'm happy just watching everybody!"

However, I could see that this clearly was not the case. Becky was looking longingly towards the pool, as she sat following the actions of everyone jumping into the water. And when I looked up, I saw them all standing in a row on the diving deck, holding hands ready to take a running jump into the deep end. Sara had a firm hold of Blake's hand on one side and Jack's hand on the other and was calling out, "One, two, three…" after which they all took a flying leap. It looked like so much fun and I was keen to join them myself.

Just then, an idea popped into my head. I whispered quietly in Millie's ear and then indicated for her to follow my lead.

Leaping to my feet, I raced to the side of the pool and called out, "Girls, have a look at this!"

Millie ran over to see what had got my attention and as expected, Becky joined her. When both girls were looking curiously into the water, wondering what I had become so excited about, I sneaked behind the two of them and pushed them both in. Becky was still fully clothed, but I was determined that she should join in the fun. The squeal of surprise that came from her just before she hit the water made everyone look in her direction.

Panicking momentarily at what her reaction would be, I let out a huge sigh of relief when she came to the surface with a grin and exclaimed, "Julia Jones! I'm going to have to get you back for that!"

"Oh well," I replied. "You're all wet now, so you may as well stay in the water!" And I dived in beside her.

Being dressed in shorts and a little singlet top, I knew Becky would be fine to swim as she was. And because we had all brought a change of clothes, I figured she'd have something dry to put on afterwards.

It turned out to be the best thing I could have done as from that moment on, the beaming smile never left her face. And it took very little effort to encourage her to join us in lining up on the diving deck ready for a big jump. She was obviously feeling comfortable as she was fully clothed rather than having to expose her body in a pair of swimmers. But I was glad to see her joining in with the rest of us.

Jackie's mom was there with her camera, ready to take photos and just as we were about to run and leap, I felt someone come around behind me and grab my hand. Looking up in surprise, I saw that it was Blake and laughing, we all held hands and took a running jump.

When we resurfaced, I noticed Sara watching as Blake tried to dunk my head under the water. She was clearly not impressed that he was showing me so much attention and then out of the blue, she suddenly starting screaming, "Oh my head! My head!" All eyes were then abruptly focused on her.

"What's wrong?" Jackie called out in a worried tone. "Are you alright Sara?"

"No!" she replied angrily. "Someone kicked me in the head when I went under water just then! Ouch, it really hurts!"

And she stormed out of the pool and slumped down in a chair in the gazebo.

Everyone else immediately climbed out and went to surround her. Jackie's mom raced inside to get some ice and some of the girls wrapped a towel around her shoulders while trying to comfort her. Millie looked at me and rolled her eyes. "What a drama queen!" she said, shaking her head as she got out of the water and headed towards the trampoline.

I looked back at Sara with puzzlement then decided she had enough people attending to her so I joined Millie on the trampoline. We soon became so absorbed in the fun we were having that we didn't realize everyone was leaving the pool area to go inside.

But when a shrill scream abruptly emanated from the direction of the house, we both looked up with a start. "Oh, my gosh!" I exclaimed to Millie. "What was that?"

Anxiously, I jumped off the trampoline and hurriedly followed her towards all the commotion.

The slumber party is hijacked...

The girls were all cowering in a corner of the living room but the reaction from the boys was completely the opposite.

"Oh, wow!" Jack was exclaiming in an excited tone. "This is awesome!"

Hovering as close as they dared to get, they stood transfixed with fascination as they stared agape at the writhing creature that had appeared on the living room floor.

"No, it is not awesome! It is totally freaky!!" Sara's squeal was the loudest of all and was probably the scream that Millie and I had heard when we were out by the pool.

Jackie's parents were nowhere to be seen and then I remembered watching them carry buckets of horse feed over to the back paddock after tending to the bump on Sara's head. So I guessed they were still over there, feeding the horses.

"Have you got a broom?' I asked Jackie as I stood in the doorway, watching the scene in front of me unfold.

It was clear that if something wasn't done quickly, one of the boys was sure to be bitten. The snake that had appeared on the rug in front of us seemed to be getting more agitated by the minute.

Jackie raced to grab a broom which I abruptly grabbed from her hands and held out towards the snake hoping to keep it at bay. We caught a glimpse of the bright red of its underbelly, which contrasted vividly with the shining black scales that covered its back.

Motioning for the girls to move out of the doorway, I tried to coax the snake towards the exit and freedom. Meanwhile, Jackie's cat sat ready to pounce, bristles raised in defense.

The screaming of the girls suddenly reached an all-time high as the snake slithered towards freedom, obviously wanting to escape the chaos that it had been faced with. Sara turned into a blubbering mess, squealing uncontrollably at the sight of the scary looking creature in front of her.

"Sara, stop screaming!" Jack exclaimed. "The snake will freak out and strike at you!"

Those were the words that she needed to hear and they actually managed to stop all the girls from carrying on in such an over the top frightened manner.

"Our cat often brings snakes into the house!" Jackie explained, trying to calm everyone down. "The other week he even dropped one on the lounge chair right next to my brother!"

Sara cried. "How on earth can you live in a place like this?"

"You've got to be kidding?" Alex replied in an amazed tone. "This is the best place ever! I'd love to live here!"

The expression on Sara's face quickly changed from horror to humiliation. Rather than giving her sympathy and attention, she was being made to seem pretty silly for reacting so foolishly. And then when she saw Blake high-five me and congratulate my quick thinking, her face glowed redder than ever.

"Oh, whatever!" she replied. "So, I'm scared of snakes. Isn't that pretty normal?"

Once again, Millie rolled her eyes towards me and then thankfully, Jackie broke the tension by inviting everyone into the dining room for something to eat. Her mom had prepared an amazing array of food, which was waiting for us on the table and as we were all starving, we eagerly sat down to enjoy the feast.

"That was really cool!" Blake exclaimed once more, glancing admiringly in my direction. "The only place I've ever seen a snake before is behind a thick pane of glass at the zoo. I never thought I'd see one up that close and especially on a living room floor. Do you think it was poisonous?"

We all looked towards Jackie, who we assumed would know something about it. "I think it was a red-bellied black snake," Jackie replied. "And yeah, they're really venomous. Our cat has definitely used up several of his nine lives since he was born, he's so lucky he hasn't ever been bitten."

"That was so awesome!" Alex commented again. And we all sat there munching away hungrily as we chatted about the excitement we had just witnessed.

Sara remained pretty quiet until we had finished eating and then someone suggested that Jackie should open her presents.

It was at that moment that Sara had a sharp change of mood. "Yes, I can't wait to see what Jackie's been given!"

She looked smugly around the group as we all left the dining table and headed out to the veranda, where the pile of wrapped presents waited to be opened.

"Save mine till last," Sara stated firmly, as she nudged it out of Jackie's reach.

As we sat watching, Jackie opened her gifts and we looked on with admiration at the lovely things she had been given. There was a gorgeous bracelet, a really cool hand bag, some cute pj's for the summer months, an iTunes gift card and some gift vouchers. The boys had chosen to give her some cash so that she could choose something for herself.

Millie and I were really pleased to see how much she loved our gift and also that the jacket fitted her so perfectly. She was especially pleased with the J pendant necklace that we had bought for her and she smiled at us gratefully.

"I've always loved your necklace, Julia and now I have one of my own! Thank you so much girls!" and she gave us each a big hug.

"Ok, now for Sara's gift," she exclaimed, smiling towards Sara questioningly. "I wonder what could possibly be inside this huge box."

We sat with anticipation, each of us wondering exactly the same thing. As I glanced at Sara, I could see that her smile really couldn't have become any wider as she waited expectantly for Jackie to open her present.

"Wow!!!" Jackie sighed in absolute astonishment as she removed the lid. Inside were several individually wrapped presents sitting decoratively amongst some pretty lilac tissue paper that had been scrunched up. As Jackie opened each parcel, the oohs and aahs from all of us looking on, continued with the unwrapping of each little gift.

There was a set of lip gloss, each one a different flavor, a box of expensive chocolates, a double pass to the cinema in town, a really pretty halter top and pair of shorts in contrasting colors and a gorgeous necklace that certainly was prettier than the simple J pendant that Millie and I had given her.

Just then, Jackie's parents arrived and the look of amazement on her mom's face echoed our thoughts completely. "Oh, my gosh, Jackie! You are such a lucky young lady! You've been given so many beautiful gifts. And are those the things that came out of that box?"

When Jackie nodded her head in acknowledgement, her mom continued, "Sara, you have really spoilt her. That was very naughty of you!" she exclaimed.

"Thank you so much, Sara!" Jackie hugged her tightly and then sat back looking at her gifts with huge delight.

"Oh, that's ok, Jackie!" Sara exclaimed modestly. "I'm glad that you like them!"

Shaking my head in wonder, I looked towards Millie whose eyes were still as wide as saucers at the sight of the extremely generous gift Sara had brought.

Then the silence that had enveloped all of us, was abruptly broken when Jackie's mom announced that it was time for birthday cake. Crowding together around Jackie for photos while her dad lit the candles, we all donned huge smiles as we called out, "Happy Birthday, Jackie!" We followed this by singing happy birthday to her and then sat down to the most delicious birthday cake I think I have ever tasted.

Soon after…as the sun was starting to set, it was time for the boys to leave. All the girls were staying for a slumber party. Jackie's parents had set up a tent in their back yard and had even gathered wood for a campfire. It was going to be the best night ever!

Jackie's Dad started the fire and we all sat around and sang songs. Then he brought out some marshmallows. We put them on sticks and toasted them in the fire. They were so delicious and it was really cool being able to sit there watching them gently sizzle over the flames.

We were all too full to eat much of the pizza they had ordered in, so we decided to play hide and seek in the dark. The laughter coming from everyone was mixed with squeals and yelps from some of the girls who were racing around on the grass. Then, all of a sudden, Millie said that she thought she could hear someone crying.

Glancing in the direction of the sobbing, I spotted Sara crouched into a ball and totally freaking out. We'd all forgotten about the snake, but she hadn't and she was actually shaking with genuine fear. I felt sorry for her, so I suggested we go back to the campfire where it was warm and not quite so dark.

"No, I want to go inside!" she cried in response.

We all looked at each other and sighed. It was clear that she was not going to be convinced to stay outdoors and when she reached the safety of Jackie's bedroom, she refused to come back out again. There was no alternative except for us all to traipse back down to the tent, bring our sleeping bags into the house along with Sara's and set them up on the lounge room floor.

"What are we going to do now?" asked Millie, her voice barely masking her disappointment.

"I know what we can do!" Sara replied with sudden enthusiasm. "How about some girly stuff? I brought my make-up kit so we can have heaps of fun with that! There's some really pretty blue eye shadow that would definitely suit the color of your eyes, Millie. Let's get it out and have a look. You girls can use whatever you want."

"Seriously, who brings their make-up kit to a slumber party?" This was the thought that was going through my head. But Sara's excited ramblings continued.

"Then we can borrow Jackie's hair dryer and straightener and straighten each other's hair!" she exclaimed with absolute delight. "I love straightening my hair, it looks so much better when I do!"

"Could this really be happening?" I shook my head in disbelief at the scene unfolding right in front of me.

"How did we go from camping with a campfire and running around in the dark, to putting on make-up and doing our hair? Don't get me wrong, I like to play around with make-up and make my hair look good, but we can do that anytime!"

I had to give her credit though! She was so good at manipulating situations to make herself happy and the center of attention. However, Jackie looked torn. It was obvious she didn't want to upset Sara but I could see by her false smile that she wasn't at all happy her slumber party had been hijacked.

To try and save the situation, I ran to get my iPod and put

on some cool music. Then, within minutes, everyone was settled around Sara's make-up and had begun testing the different products that were stored in the large pink carry case.

The music certainly helped to lift everyone's spirits as well and before long, we were all singing to our favorite hit songs.

I was pleased to see that Jackie was laughing once again and having fun. There would be nothing worse than to have your party spoiled by one of your guests. But as it turned out, we all had a pretty good time.

The next morning, after very little sleep because Sara was too scared to close her eyes in case the snake came back, we dragged ourselves out of our sleeping bags so that we could head into the dining room for breakfast. Sara's mom had made pancakes and we sat around the table in our pajamas, talking and laughing about how much fun the party had been.

Unfortunately though, everyone's parents soon started to arrive and it was time to head home. Before leaving though, we all agreed to try and fit in as many dance practices as possible during the next few days at school. The final dress rehearsal was scheduled for later in the week and we still had lots of work to do before then.

As Millie and I hopped into the back of my dad's car, I overheard Sara commenting to some of the girls. "I can't wait for the musical! It's going to be amazing and I'm sure everyone will be in for a huge surprise!"

Just as I closed the door, I caught her glancing in our direction but the strange expression on her face carried a meaning that I couldn't quite fathom. She waved as we drove off but the cold look was what worried me the most.

Regardless of the party being hijacked by Sara, we had still thoroughly enjoyed it and now the musical was quickly approaching. I should have been full of excited anticipation but the sudden attack of nerves that I had been overcome with, caught me by surprise. Feeling tired and a little anxious, I leaned back against the head rest on the rear seat of the car and closed my eyes.

Oh no, NOT today....

The eve of the musical finally dawned and I had gone to bed early in order to get a good night's sleep. Our dress rehearsal had been a roaring success with every single item being performed almost to perfection. Miss Sheldon was beside herself with excitement. She seemed to think that it looked to be the best show the school had ever performed. At least since she had been teaching there, and she had huge expectations of a stand out extravaganza.

The tickets had all sold out and the office staff were asked to quickly print extras as well as hire more chairs to squash into the already very crowded auditorium. This was necessary to accommodate the overwhelming number of people who were keen to be a part of the audience. It appeared that almost half the town were coming and it was just lucky that the hall was big enough to seat everyone.

I rolled over in bed and closed my eyes, determined to fall asleep quickly so that the morning would arrive and I could begin the exciting day ahead. Then, what seemed like only a few minutes later, I was awakened by a noise outside my bedroom door.

Sitting up, I realized that it was our dog, Roxy scratching at the door and trying to get in. As I rubbed my eyes in an attempt to focus, I became aware of daylight streaming into the room from behind my curtain.

Glancing at the alarm clock that sat on the bedside table next to my bed, I rubbed my eyes once more. With a sick feeling in the pit of my stomach, I grabbed hold of the clock and looked at the time again.

"Noooo!" I screamed loudly. "This can't be happening!"

I slept in!

With my heart racing like the beat of a pounding drum, I frantically sprinted out of bed, opened the door and looked out into the hallway. Ignoring the eager tail wagging and expectant look from Roxy, I bounded towards the bathroom and turned the handle of the door. But it wouldn't budge.

"Oh no!" I grumbled loudly, then heard the familiar sound of my brother singing in the shower. "I need the shower!" I yelled desperately. "Hurry up!!!"

Of all mornings to have slept in! I just couldn't believe that my alarm hadn't gone off. I was sure that I had set it accurately the night before, thinking at the time I certainly didn't want to risk oversleeping and missing my bus.

"The bus! Oh, my gosh!" I yelled, running back into my bedroom to double check the time. The early bus was due in five minutes and there was no way I could get a lift to school. Because my parents both had a seven o'clock start on a Friday morning, I knew that they would have already left for work. I thought about my promise to Miss Sheldon, agreeing I would arrive early to help with all the setting up which still had to be done. It was blatantly obvious that I needed to get to school as soon as possible.

Deciding to go without a morning shower as I'd had one the night before, I threw on my clothes and grabbed the bag that

I had already packed ready with everything I would need to take. Bolting down the stairs, I literally flew out the front door.

I don't think I have ever sprinted as fast as I did that morning. But to my huge dismay, I arrived at the bus stop out of breath, only to see the bus pulling away from the curb. Yelling for the driver to stop, was a waste of time and I anxiously watched the bus head down the street.

Dropping my bag on the ground in disgust, I stood there in despair racking my brains for a solution. Waiting for the next bus was not an option; that would get me to school just before the bell and I needed to arrive much earlier than that, in order to get all the necessary jobs done.

It was then I decided that I would have to walk. A fast walk along with running some of the way, would be the quickest alternative. And besides that, I was too worked up to stand there waiting 40 minutes for the next bus to arrive.

So off I took and just when I realized that I was actually making pretty good time, I felt some droplets of water on my face. Looking up, I spotted an accumulation of very dark clouds heading my way so even though I was already breathless, I forced myself to run.

However, I was unable to beat the rain. At first it was a light sprinkle and then gradually became slightly heavier. Within minutes though, it was bucketing down and I was absolutely drenched.

Running through the school gates and trying to avoid a huge puddle of water that sat right in the middle of the driveway, the rubber bottom of my shoe skidded wildly. Feeling as though I was skating on ice, I slid recklessly across the slippery surface, desperately trying to maintain my balance. But then with an uncontrollable yelp, my legs went out from under me.

I hit the hard asphalt with a thud, landing flat on my back, my head coming down heavily with a bang. Dazed and very sore, I managed to stand, the rain still pouring down around me. By this time, I was absolutely saturated and had mud all over me along with a scraped and bleeding knee. I could already feel the throbbing lump starting to form on my head and I hobbled cautiously towards the Performing Arts building, not wanting to slip over again.

When I entered, the room was full of excitement and noise. People were scattered all over the place in various stages of preparation. I ducked under a ladder that was blocking the entrance and looked up to see Blake helping to hang a large banner.

"Not a good idea to walk under ladders, Julia," Miss Sheldon warned when she noticed me trying to weave my way inside the door. "That brings bad luck you know!"

"As if I haven't already had enough bad luck today!" I muttered miserably to myself.

Then all of a sudden she did an abrupt double take. "Julia!" she exclaimed in a worried tone. "You're soaking wet! And what have you done to yourself?" She looked down at the blood oozing from the graze on my leg which now appeared much nastier than I had originally thought.

I could feel tears starting to form in the corners of my eyes but then noticed Blake climbing down the ladder towards me so I quickly brushed them away.

"I'm alright," I said trying to muster a convincing tone. "I missed the bus, so I decided to walk to school. But it started to pour with rain and then I slipped on a puddle in the school driveway."

"I'll get a first aid kit," Miss Sheldon quickly replied. "I don't really like the look of that gash on the side of your knee. I hope it doesn't need stitches!"

"Oh, I'm sure it'll be fine," I said bravely, as I took a sip of water from the bottle that Blake had handed me.

"Blake, see if you can get something to press onto that gash and stop the bleeding. I'll be back in a minute." Miss Sheldon raced towards her office, on the way picking up a roll of paper toweling that had been left on a chair. "Here you go, use this," and she threw it towards him.

I sat down while Blake held strips of the toweling firmly on my leg as I miserably watched pools of water dripping onto the floor around me. In no time though, Miss Sheldon was back and had cleaned the wound with antiseptic and wrapped my leg in a sterile bandage.

"It looks like you fell on something sharp," she commented. "We'll have to keep an eye on that. But in the meantime, why don't you try and dry off. There's some towels in the cupboard in my office and there might be some clothes in there that you can change into."

"Thank you, Miss Sheldon!" I replied gratefully. "I actually have a change of clothes with me. And at least my back pack

is waterproof, otherwise everything would be completely soaked, including my costume for tonight."

Millie then spotted me and raced over, a worried expression on her face. Rubbing my head tenderly, and wincing with pain, I explained what had happened.

When she realized that along with everything else, I also had a huge lump on my head, she ran to get some ice from the kitchen and then grabbed a couple of towels from the cupboard in Miss Sheldon's office.

After putting on dry clothes, I gratefully accepted a cup of hot chocolate and a breakfast bagel that had been provided for everyone who had offered to help that morning.

Holding the ice pack to my head, I looked down at the tight

bandaging on my leg and hoped that it wouldn't restrict my dance moves. "Maybe I can just take the bandage off later," I said to Millie. "The bleeding will have stopped by then and at least I'll have more freedom of movement!"

She looked at me with sympathy and commented in her usual positive manner, "Well, thank goodness you got here, Julia! The show just couldn't go on without you!"

Grateful for her caring friendship, I smiled warmly and sipped the soothing drink which was helping to make me feel much better. Then with a determined resolve, I got to my feet and set myself to work. There was lots to be done and I knew that I needed to get started. We had a show to perform and nothing was going to stop it from being the best show ever. We had all worked so hard and I knew that it had to be a roaring success!

I spent the morning helping as much as I could. Although the throbbing pain I was feeling in my head had seemed to intensify, I focused my thoughts on the celebrations we would be having later that night, over the wonderful show we had performed.

And then suddenly out of the corner of my eye, I saw Sara Hamilton walk into the room.

Overwhelmed...

"Oh, Julia!" Sara wailed, as she headed in my direction. "I just heard about your accident. Will you be able to dance tonight?"

"Yes, I'll be fine," I abruptly assured her.

"Are you sure?" she asked, exhibiting what looked like a semblance of sympathy. "I wondered if you might be out of action! That would be such a terrible shame after all your hard work."

"Nothing will keep me off that stage tonight, Sara!" I declared in a determined voice.

"I thought it would have to be something terrible for you not to perform," Sara responded. "After all, you're pretty much the star of the show, of the dancing segments, anyway."

"Sara you have the lead role in our dance now, but regardless, it's a team effort and I think everyone will be stars tonight," I stated firmly.

I really wasn't in the mood for her games and hidden meanings. I just wanted to focus on getting organized and right then, I had a splitting headache and a really stiff and sore knee.

"By the way," Sara added. "Miss Fitz wants to see you. It's about the headbands for the girls' hair that you were meant to bring with you today."

"The headbands?" I asked, a sinking feeling forming in the pit of my stomach.

"Yeah," Sara replied. "Remember I gave you the message

from Miss Fitz yesterday afternoon? She arranged for your neighbor to do some last minute sewing and you were meant to bring them with you to school today."

"Sara, I don't remember you telling me that," I said, looking at her in complete puzzlement.

"You'd better go and see Miss Fitz," she replied. "She's freaking out in there because a lot of people haven't followed through with various commitments that they're responsible for. Miss Fitz and Miss Sheldon are complaining that some of the committee members should have been more organized."

Approaching her office apprehensively, I could see as I entered that Miss Fitz appeared quite stressed. "Miss Fitz," I stammered hesitatingly. "Sara said that you wanted to see me."

"Julia, please tell me that you brought those head pieces to school with you today?" We need them to keep the girls' hair pinned back. That dance that you choreographed for them has their hair flopping around everywhere and this is the last finishing touch."

"I know they need them, Miss Fitz but I wasn't aware that I was responsible for collecting them."

Just as she was about to take a deep breath and probably let fly with an angry retort, I asked if I could use the phone to call my mom. "She should be able to call in and pick them up," I explained hopefully.

"OK, and please be quick, there's still lots to do!"

Sighing with relief, I put the phone down a few minutes later. Mom had agreed to get the head pieces. I just prayed that our neighbor was at home. I knew that she usually headed off to visit her sister on Friday afternoons and often stayed there for dinner. But hopefully she might have left them out for someone to collect.

I crossed my fingers and sneaked out of the office, deciding that I should stay out of the way of my drama teacher. But I understood how stressful the whole situation was. Organizing something that was the magnitude of our school musical was a mammoth task and any number of things could go wrong.

Thinking again of Sara's words, I tried to recall her mentioning the message the day before but had no memory of it whatsoever. "Am I really becoming that forgetful?" I wondered. "Or is there just too much on my mind right now?"

As I thought about it some more, desperately searching through my memory banks, I could not bring myself to recollect Sara giving me the message from Miss Fitz.

Looking in Sara's direction, I could see her in a corner of the hall, laughing with Blake and some of the other boys. They were obviously enjoying her company and she was definitely thriving on the attention they were giving her.

She must have felt my eyes on her because she abruptly glanced my way and then with a little smirk, turned her back on me to refocus on the group of boys once more.

A feeling of doubt started to weave its way through my mind and tingles of apprehension began to build. Trying to force the worried thoughts away, I headed towards Millie and a group of other girls who were busy with the list of jobs that still had to be done.

Still absorbed in my thoughts, I failed to notice a wooden box that had been left lying in the middle of the floor. It was only small and the tawny brown color blended in with the floorboards beneath it. I didn't realize it was there until it was too late and I felt myself suddenly being propelled into mid-air. Desperately trying to regain my balance, I let out a loud yelp. This is something I have a bad habit of doing and rather than avoiding attention, it always alerts everyone around me. Of course, this occasion, was no different from any other and my squeal of fright drew all eyes towards me.

Landing heavily on top of the box, I could not stop the tears that began to flow down my cheeks. The humiliation and embarrassment of everyone staring at me and rushing to see if I was ok, was just too much to bear; that and the sharp pain that was added to my already throbbing leg. But the worst part of all was Sara's voice over all the others, "Oh my gosh, Julia! What is wrong with you today? I hope you don't fall over in our dance tonight! Are you sure you're going to be alright to perform?"

Throwing a black look in her direction, I didn't trust myself to reply for fear of bursting into a crying fit and embarrassing myself even more.

As Millie helped me to my feet and then to a nearby chair, the feeling of overwhelm that had engulfed me was like a bottomless pit I was frantically trying to climb out of.

The day I had been looking forward to for so long, had gone from bad to worse and I desperately hoped that no more terrible things would happen!

A Math Comp, of all things...

"You'll be fine, Julia," Millie said in her usual cheery voice. "Everything will go perfectly well tonight, you just wait and see!" I looked gratefully at my friend, very much wanting her to be right.

I had no time to focus on it any further though as there was still so much to do and to add to that, some of us had to be back in class straight after the morning tea break. A group of kids from our grade had been selected to enter a state-wide Math competition which just happened to be scheduled for the same day as the musical. This had been an oversight by our teacher who hadn't realized that the musical was also on that day. But because she had arranged for the school to pay the administration fee for each of the entrants, we were expected to be there. She gave us the condition that if we wanted to have the day off class to help out with the musical, then we had to do the Math comp.

"It's not fair," complained Millie as we hurried to the classroom where the competition was to be held. "This wasn't our choice! Why couldn't it just be left to all the math nerds in our grade? Why did they have to include us as well?"

"I think they were short of kids to enter," I replied. "But Math is my worst subject. I can't figure out why they chose me."

"Even though it's your worst subject, you're still good at it!" Millie exclaimed. "Better than me, anyway!"

"I thought this day couldn't get any worse!" That was the last thought in my mind before I sat down to focus on the paper in front of me. Rolling my eyes and sighing with impatience, I decided just to do the work and get it finished as soon as possible. We had planned one last rehearsal with our dance troupe and I was keen to get back to the buzzing excitement in the hall. Attempting to ignore my throbbing leg as well as the pain coming from the lump on my head, I looked down towards the Math questions on my desk and tried to concentrate.

Not feeling at all well...

Can things get any worse?...

Rushing back to the hall afterwards, Millie and I complained about the hard Math questions that had been included, especially towards the very end. The last few were so complicated.

"I skipped several of them," I admitted. "They were way too hard! And I'm certainly not looking forward to getting my result, that's for sure! If we're ever asked to do one of those competitions again, I'm just going to refuse!"

Millie agreed with me but on entering the hall, we quickly put the Math comp behind us. The seating and decorations were finally all in place and Miss Sheldon was directing a group of kids on the stage who were having a last minute rehearsal.

I scanned the hall, looking for all the members of our dance troupe so that we could also have a final rehearsal. We'd been discussing it that morning and had planned to meet up just after the lunch break, but they were nowhere to be seen.

"Maybe they're all out the back or in the dressing rooms. I'll race out and have a look." I watched Millie head off to look for them and just as I was about to search the adjoining rehearsal room, Miss Sheldon called me over. "Julia!" she said, "Just the person I was looking for!"

"Yes, Miss?" I replied questioningly.

"I'd like you to come with me. The junior girls need a last minute practice and I also need you to help me with the Grade Five item. There's still kids who could do with some extra help and I think one more run through is really going to benefit them."

The look of dismay on my face must have been obvious. "Aren't you feeling well?" she queried. "Is your leg a problem? Perhaps you should be at home resting it!"

"Oh no," I replied quickly. "My leg is fine." There was no way I was going to tell her that it was actually quite painful.

If I did, I was worried that she'd ban me from performing.

"I was just going to have a last rehearsal with the kids in my dance group," I tried to explain, but her stressed expression prevented me from continuing. "It's ok, though! I know the dance really well, they can just go ahead without me."

Trying to sound convincing, I followed her into the rehearsal room where the group of junior girls were waiting. I thought anxiously of Millie and the others, knowing they would be wondering where I was but I didn't dare leave to go and tell them. Miss Sheldon was a great teacher, but when she was stressed or angry, we all knew we just had to be quiet and do as we were told.

Thankfully, it didn't take long to get the junior girls in order and by the second run through, they had pretty much perfected the mistakes they'd been making. With a huge sigh I then moved onto the Grade Five kids, many of whom were racing crazily around the hall by that stage.

There were some pretty hyperactive boys in that group and they could not sit still, let alone follow instructions and it took all my strength not to start yelling at them to be quiet and listen. I was relieved when Miss Sheldon came over and told them off. That finally managed to calm them down and we were able to run through their entire item.

Just as we finished and I was about to go and look for Millie and the others, I heard an unmistakable voice. "Julia, where have you been?" We've been working our butts off trying to get our dance perfect and you didn't even bother to show up! Do you want our dance to be a success or not?"

The uncomfortable looks on the faces of all the others, just added to my humiliation. "I had to help Miss Sheldon," I tried to explain.

"Yeah, right!" I could feel my face turning bright red at Sara's abrupt remarks. "You're such a teacher's pet! You'll do anything to get on side with the teachers, even if it means letting your team down. Unbelievable!" And with a flick of her long blonde hair, she strode off towards the change rooms.

I looked towards Millie who just rolled her eyes and said, "Don't worry about her, Julia. You know the dance so well, we'll be great tonight, let's just go and get ready."

Feeling upset for what seemed like the umpteenth time that day, I slowly walked towards the change room door. I knew that the junior school kids were opening the show and I needed to be back stage to help them into their costumes. Taking a deep breath, I tried to muster some enthusiasm as I entered the bustling room that was filled with girls at different stages of preparation.

I suddenly looked at my watch. Seeing a few girls in the midst of getting their hair and make-up done, reminded me of the missing head bands and I anxiously hoped that my mother would make it in time.

The girls were expecting to wear the head pieces and apart from the decorative effect they created, they really were needed to help keep their hair tied back. With the throbbing in my head becoming worse, I walked over to the dressing area to assist the remaining girls with their costumes and make-up.

When they were finally organized, I decided I had better get dressed myself. If I didn't hurry, I would never be ready on time.

Searching frantically for my back pack, I scoured the area where I thought I had left it when I had arrived that morning. My memory of the morning's events was pretty foggy and I couldn't remember exactly where I had placed my bag. The change room was in chaos at that point. There were girls, teachers and helpers everywhere. Everyone was at different stages of getting ready and Mrs. Jackson was trying to keep the noise to a minimum.

"Sssshhhh, girls!" she was saying in a firm voice. "Please keep your voices down. It is way too noisy in here!"

By that stage, the room was totally frantic with excitement, the big night had finally arrived and girls in tutus, leotards and a variety of different costumes were lining up to get their make-up and hair done. I thought fleetingly about the head pieces for the younger girls and looked with concern at the clock on the wall, hoping that my mom would soon arrive.

"Millie," I called, when I spotted her and the other girls from our dance group assisting each other with applying mascara and lipstick.

"Can you please help me find my bag? I'm sure I left it in here this morning after getting changed, but I can't see it anywhere."

"Julia! I was wondering where you were and look at you! You're not even dressed yet. You need to hurry!" Millie's worried look made me feel even more anxious.

There were bags and costumes and props scattered all over the place, it was no wonder I couldn't see my bag but after a few minutes of searching, Millie finally handed it to me, "Here it is! I found it hidden under a pile of gear in that corner over there."

Frowning, I answered, "I could have sworn I left it over by the door."

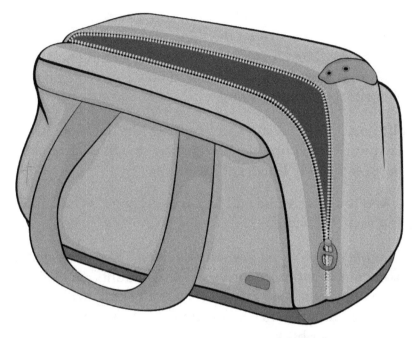

Millie shook her head and said, "Everything is such a mess in here. I'm surprised I found it at all!"

Casting my confusion aside, I quickly rifled through my bag, looking for the hip hop outfit that I had carefully folded and placed in there the night before, along with my shoes and accessories. But to my horror, it quickly became obvious that the outfit was missing.

Pulling everything out, I threw each item singly onto the floor, desperately hoping that the clothes I needed were hidden amongst my other bits and pieces. At the bottom of my bag, were my shoes and the long socks that we had all planned to wear, but there was no sign of the outfit I was looking for.

"NO!!!" I cried out.

"What's wrong, Julia?" Jackie had heard my distressed call and came over to see what the problem was.

"My clothes aren't in here! But I'm sure I packed them last night!" I flopped down on the floor, tears springing from my eyes. The day I had looked forward to for so long had gone from bad to worse. And I wondered how everything could have gone so terribly wrong.

"Fifteen minutes till show time, girls!" Mrs. Jackson was calling out. "I will need to start getting you lined up in your groups, so quickly finish getting ready.

I looked towards Millie and Jackie in despair. "What am I going to do?" I wailed.

"Julia Jones, aren't you even dressed yet?" Mrs. Jackson was looking at me with an expression of incredulity on her face. "Hurry up! There's no time to waste!" Shaking her head, she turned her attention to some younger girls who were trying to pin their hair back.

"Aren't these girls supposed to be wearing head pieces?" she asked no one in particular.

I didn't respond to that, thinking that I had much more important things to worry about than the girls' hair. How on earth was I going to be able to go on stage without my costume?

"What's wrong, Julia?" Sara's voice rang in my ears. "You're still not dressed! Have you decided not to perform?"

I was sure that her tone was full of sarcasm but as I turned to face her, I couldn't help but notice how pretty she looked.

Her glowing blonde hair was slicked back into a high pony tail and the bright red lipstick adorning her lips, set off her olive complexion beautifully. She looked so good in the outfit that had been designed for us all, and I felt overwhelmed with disappointment at the thought of not being able to take part.

"Julia, you can wear this!" the unexpected sight of the familiar shimmering blue fabric in Millie's hands was the answer to my prayers.

"Oh, Millie! Where did you find it?" I asked, barely daring to breathe.

"This one belongs to Annie Thompson. When she broke her leg, she returned it to Miss Sheldon and I spotted it in the cupboard in her office when I went looking for towels this morning."

"Oh, my gosh, Millie!" I said gratefully. "You're a life saver!"

I glanced in Sara's direction and noticed the surprised look on her face. "Looks like I'll be going on after all, Sara." I said in a curt tone and quickly rushed to get changed.

I tried not to think about the throbbing pain still emanating from my head as well as the gash on my knee. I had pulled the blood soaked bandage off and although my leg really needed to be covered up, I couldn't very well go on stage with a horrible looking bandage wrapped around it.

By the time I was dressed, there was no time to worry about make-up. I swiftly tied my hair back into a pony tail and regardless of the fact that it wasn't as neat as I would normally like, it just simply had to do.

Disaster...

After directing the younger girls onto the stage for their opening dance, I took a deep breath and watched from the wings, praying that even without their head pieces, they would exhibit the same killer performance that they had in the rehearsal.

The deafening applause at the end of their dance was music to my ears and I congratulated them all as they skipped off the stage.

The next act was performed by Liam, and his incredible voice poured out into the auditorium.

The other singers were almost as good and I marveled once again at the talented kids in our school.

The following performances were met with just as much enthusiasm from the audience. Then peering out into the crowd, I spotted my parents and my brother, Matt sitting near the front row. I assumed that my mom hadn't been able to get the head pieces, but as it turned out, the girls managed to get through their dance regardless, so I was very grateful for that. Although I still felt bad over their obvious disappointment at not being able to wear the sparkling addition to their costumes.

Finally, it was our turn and my stomach churned with anxiety and nerves. As we raced out onto the stage to form our positions before the curtain went up, Sara turned to me and said, "Break a leg, Julia!"

"What?" I frowned.

"That's for good luck," she smirked and then faced the audience whose applause was deafening once again.

We lunged into our routine, with Sara in the front row, doing the somersaults that she was so good at and as usual, her precision and timing were excellent. The applause erupted again and with a flick of her long pony tail, she executed a very tricky interchange with Alex and then moved to the back.

Alex attacked his moves with his usual gusto and the sharp, expressive movements which made him the stand out hip hop dancer that he was. I felt a rush of pride at being a part of such a cool routine but just as I moved to the front position, I felt my leg give way under me.

It was a completely involuntary reaction and one I was powerless to prevent. I was supposed to kneel down and support the weight of one of the smaller girls on my bent knee but unfortunately it was the leg that I had injured that morning.

There was no way I could bear her weight and the sharp pain caused my knee to drop just as Abbie pressed down on it to raise herself into the air. With a gasp from the audience, she went tumbling to the ground. Bright red with embarrassment, she glared at me in horror and all I could do was help her up and try to resume the timing and movements of the routine going on around us.

Fortunately, Abbie had no trouble getting back into rhythm, but I just seemed to lose my place and was not able to recover. As if in slow motion, I felt myself limping around the stage after the others and then looking down, I realized that blood was oozing from my leg and onto the floor.

I tried to ignore it and focus on the moves that I knew so well, but I was simply unable to get it together. Gratefully, Millie took over my spot and I moved once again to the back row, trying to camouflage myself amongst the others.

The scene around me was almost surreal and I felt as though I were a spectator watching the event unfold from afar. The swirling, twisting and turning of the dancers in front of me, along with the steady thumping beat of the latest hip hop song that everyone knew so well, all seemed to mesh together into a whirlpool of crazy colors and sounds.

Then, feeling a slight nudge in my lower back, I was pushed towards the front of the stage. An instant flash of recall had me leaping into the air.

Everyone still considered this moment the highlight of our routine. It was the grand finale and my chance to relinquish my status as actually being a decent dancer and choreographer.

Flinging my arms and legs forward, I came down onto the stage, one foot at a time. Then reminiscent of that morning's episode in the school driveway, rather than gripping onto the stage in a final dramatic stomp, my foot slid forward and just kept on going until my whole body landed horizontally on the floor with a loud bang.

In a blur of dizziness, I sat up and looked around then saw that I had slipped on a pool of blood; blood that had oozed from the gash in my knee and onto the stage. At that very moment, I was overcome with a sudden rush of nausea and unable to stop the sudden convulsion, I vomited all over the floor in front of me.

Too terrified to open my eyes, I wished I could turn back the

clock. Back to the day of our dress rehearsal when everything had gone so smoothly. My final leap had been the high point of the day, where even Miss Sheldon and also Alex our expert hip hop dancer, had congratulated me on my performance.

I dared to glance fearfully out into the audience. Everyone appeared aghast and I could see the shocked expressions of my mom and dad. Then, realizing I was surrounded by worried faces peering down at me, everything suddenly went black.

What is Sara really up to?...

The next thing I remember was my mom's voice. "Julia, Julia!" Are you alright, darling? Julia..."

I had gazed at her briefly before blacking out once more and then awoke in a strange bed, my mom, dad and brother by my side.

After collapsing so dramatically on stage, I'd been rushed to hospital in an ambulance where I'd had to spend the night for observation.

When I opened my eyes, my mom hugged me tightly, the relief obvious in her eyes. "I'm so glad that you're ok, sweetheart!"

"You had us really worried, Julia!" my dad continued with concern.

And then of course, a typical comment from my brother, Matt. "What a finale, Julia. You were awesome!"

Mom looked at him crossly which quickly wiped the grin from his face. Trust him to try to joke around, even at the most inappropriate times. I certainly wasn't laughing but I sure was glad to have my mom and dad there with me.

When I was finally allowed to leave the hospital, I couldn't wait to get home to the safety of my room and I quickly climbed the stairs, declining any offers of help from my parents.

I could not believe that the night I had been looking forward to for so long had ended up so badly. All the time and effort I had put in to getting our dance perfect was for nothing.

Well, that's how it seemed to me. I had practiced and rehearsed constantly, just as much or even more than anyone else. And it had all ended disastrously.

After arriving home from the hospital, I spent the next 2 days in bed. I felt so embarrassed and humiliated and didn't want to face any of my friends ever again.

"Perhaps I could go to another school?" That was the question I silently asked myself over and over while trying to be brave enough to make the suggestion to my parents in the hope that it might be possible.

I knew they wouldn't allow me to change schools but I just did not know how I could possibly face everyone again. I decided that I must be the laughing stock of the grade and I really dreaded the thought of ever going back.

I replayed the entire events of that terrible day in my mind, right from the moment when I had woken up late and realized I had overslept. Thinking back now, I've come to the conclusion that it was doomed from the start. So many things went wrong and it just didn't seem fair.

As I lay there, I envisioned the smirk on Sara's face that I had seen so often. I felt totally convinced that she was not the girl I had originally thought she would be. Too many things had happened over the past weeks and I tried to piece the puzzle together.

A couple of events stood out in my mind. For one, the message from Miss Fitz about the head bands for the junior girls. I am positive that Sara never gave me that message.

Another issue was my missing costume for our dance. I'm sure that I packed it and since coming home, I've searched every possible spot in my room but it's nowhere to be seen. I know that I had it in my bag, and if that is the case then where did it get to? And where is it now?

I wondered if that mystery would ever be solved. I thought briefly about confronting Sara and asking her directly if she knew anything about it but I was sure that would be useless. She'd never admit to anything, even if she was guilty.

Just as I was trying to concoct a really good excuse for having the entire week off school, I heard a gentle knock on my door. Then to my surprise, Millie's smiling face appeared.

"Julia!" She came rushing over to my bed to give me a huge hug. "Are you ok?" she asked, with genuine concern. "I've been so worried about you! I wanted to come sooner but your mom said that you needed some time to recover before having visitors."

Just having Millie there, was instantly reassuring and I could feel my spirits rise. Then when she pulled a block of my all-time favorite chocolate out of her back pack, I couldn't help but grin widely.

"My favorite!" I exclaimed. "Thank you so much!"

"I know," she replied, watching me rip the wrapping open. "I was hoping it might cheer you up."

"It's so good to see you, Millie!" I responded, hugging her once more. "But I'm so embarrassed about what happened. How am I ever going to go back to school again?"

"Everyone was worried about you, Julia!" she quickly replied. "After the ambulance came, you were all that everyone could talk about. They were all really concerned. They'll be so happy to see you back at school tomorrow."

I looked away from her trying to hide the tears that had sprung to my eyes. "I really don't want to go back to school,

Millie. I'm so worried about seeing everyone. It's all so humiliating."

"Julia, don't be silly. Everyone will be so happy to see that you're alright. And the musical would never have happened without you. Miss Fitz and Miss Sheldon are so grateful for all your help. They even made an announcement at the end of the night and everyone stood up and cheered. They all know how hard you worked to put it all together."

At that moment, I felt especially grateful to have Millie as my friend and I glanced towards the wall where I had my favorite photos attached to a board. In particular, I loved the shot my mom had taken of us while we'd been taking our own selfie. Just the sight of that image instantly put a smile on my face.

Keen to convince me that everything was okay, Millie continued on.

"Anyway, Julia, it was lucky that our dance was the last performance. Everyone got to perform and apart from you collapsing, the show was a huge success. But so much of it was thanks to you!"

After a moment's silence, she questioned anxiously, "You ARE coming back to school tomorrow, aren't you, Julia?"

With a nod of my head, I gave her another big hug. But I was still concerned about Sara. I wasn't sure whether to mention her to Millie or not. Millie would probably say I'm imagining things and being completely silly.

I decided to keep my thoughts to myself. I didn't want to spoil Millie's visit. I was so glad that she was there and I forced myself to look forward to returning to school the following day.

Back at school...

Everyone really did seem pretty concerned when I turned up at school. A heap of kids surrounded me, asking if I was ok. The teachers all came to check on me as well.

It was so nice to see that they genuinely cared, although I really didn't want to talk about it at all. I had decided to label that day, 'My Worst Day Ever,' and I definitely wanted to put it out of my mind forever.

Some of the kids were already talking about the next musical, but I certainly was not interested in getting involved in that conversation. I think that I've had more than my share of musicals for a long time.

I avoided making eye contact with Sara during class that morning. The desks had been rearranged the week before and I was very glad not to be sitting next to her any longer. That definitely helped me to get through the morning. I just focused on my school work and tried not to think about her.

During our lunch break though, I could see Sara surrounded by her adoring fan club. That's what Millie called them anyway.

Since the musical, apparently everyone had been raving about how great her dancing was and commenting that she was the star of our routine. But I guess that was what Sara had wanted to achieve and she'd managed to get her wish.

Chatting with Millie and the others, I was glad that I had a nice group of friends whose company I could enjoy without having to feel anxious or worried about what they might do or say. That's what I needed to focus on, I tried to remind myself.

But then, without warning, I felt someone's eyes on me and turned towards the group of kids who sat huddled together in a nearby corner, absorbed in each other's animated conversation. With a sudden shiver of apprehension, I realized that Sara was staring in my direction. And I knew without doubt that she must be staring at me.

Her blue eyes were so intense right then and the look she gave was full of attitude. Draping her arm around Blake's shoulder, she pulled him close and whispered something into his ear. Her eyes never leaving mine, I saw them both laugh at her obvious joke. Feeling very uneasy, I looked nervously away.

I had no idea what was going on in her head or what had caused the animosity that she was directing towards me and the uncomfortable sensation I was feeling, continued. With a tingling of unease, I turned my back on the group and tried to refocus on the friends sitting beside me who were consumed by their own friendly chatter.

I decided that I should put Sara out of my mind. Although I wanted the mystery solved and my questions answered, I figured I should just focus on my real friends, the ones who I always felt comfortable with. And besides, perhaps it was all in my imagination.

Perhaps Sara had passed on Miss Fitz's message and I had simply forgotten about it. And perhaps my dance costume was just mislaid amongst all the chaos in the dressing room on the night of the musical.

Perhaps? Or perhaps not? I really didn't know what to think!

Then a few minutes later, from directly behind, I heard the sound of a familiar voice. "Hey, Julia! Good to see you back at school!"

As I looked towards the voice, a group of laughing girls suddenly emerged, heading in the direction of their classroom and I couldn't see who the voice had come from. I was fairly convinced that it was Sara who had spoken, but I wasn't completely sure.

The tone had been friendly enough, but I didn't know if there was a hidden meaning behind the words. Was she really happy to see me back at school or not? And was it actually Sara whose voice I had heard?

"Did you see who that was?" I asked Millie.

"Who what was?" she replied.

"I thought I heard someone talking to me," I answered thoughtfully. "But maybe I was imagining things."

Jumping tensely at the sudden shrill ring of the bell which signalled the end of lunch break, I glanced around once more. "Yes, it must have been my imagination," I repeated, looking around one last time.

Then I stood to follow Millie and the others back to class. I tried to get involved in their giggling and joking around, but I could not dispel the confused but foreboding sensation I had been overcome with.

Was Sara trying to be friendly or wasn't she? Did she have a hidden agenda or did I just have an over-active imagination?

Confused thoughts raced through my mind as I headed back to class.

Then, unexpectedly, I felt a light tap on my shoulder. Whipping my head around nervously, I gasped in surprise.

"Julia! I'm so glad to see that you're ok! We were all freaking out the other night!"

Blake's sparkling eyes and friendly smile were enough to make my heart melt.

I felt the tension ease away as we strode along the pathway and up the stairs towards our classroom, all the while chatting comfortably as we walked.

"I'm so glad I came back to school," I thought happily to myself, all thoughts of Sara disappearing temporarily from my mind.

But then I entered the room. And it was at that moment, I could feel the hairs on my arms stand on end. I looked questioningly up at Blake, who was still at my side laughing easily.

I was unsure what had caused the sudden chill I was feeling and rubbed my arms for warmth, attempting to fend off the cool draught that had abruptly appeared from nowhere.

It was when I happened to glance towards the back of the class, that I saw a pair of penetrating blue eyes drilling into my own. The expression that had crept over Sara's features was dark and forceful, but the disturbing thing was that her death-like stare was aimed directly at me.

Completely unaware of the look I was receiving, Blake left my side and sat down in his seat in the front row.

Tentatively, I made my way to my own spot and sat down, grateful to escape the wrath of her evil glare.

The uncomfortable sensation lingered however, and I was forced to turn to face her once more. Still staring directly towards me, I was sure that she had begun to shake her head. It was the slightest movement, barely noticeable, but definitely betraying a hidden meaning.

As I turned back towards the front of the room, I felt my throat become dry, while at the same time, confused and anxious thoughts flooded my mind.

Swallowing hard, I took a deep breath and tried to ease the nervous energy I had been overcome with. But for some strange reason, it continued to linger and I remained in my seat, eyes faced forward, not daring to look behind me again.

When the final bell of the day clanged loudly, I instantly stood, eager to leave the classroom as quickly as possible. But as I walked to the bus stop, I could not shake the sinking feeling that had lodged itself in the pit of my stomach.

***

What lies ahead for Julia Jones?
Will Sara be her friend or does she have something else in
store for Julia?

Find out in Book 2
Julia Jones' Diary – My Secret Bully

**Read what others are saying about Julia Jones' Diary -
Book 2...**

*-Love the book Katrina Kahler it is awesome, best book ever. I have
never read a book in 3 days and that's saying something because I
don't typically read that fast ever.*

*-This book is realistic, it's almost like I can feel it. I recommend
this book to everyone. I picked five stars because it was really
AWESOME!! It's good advice if you are getting bullied. I really
recommend this book!*

Diary of a Horse Mad Girl Book 1 - My First Pony

Dedication

This book is dedicated to my beautiful daughter. These are her adventures and we all loved going along for the ride. I hope you do too!

Hi, my name is Abbie and this diary is all about me and my very first pony, Sparkle who is a beautiful 13 hand Palomino. She is the best first pony anyone could wish for and we've had so many great adventures together. Luckily, I live on a rural property with lots of land and also other neighborhood girls to ride with. We have our very own "Saddle Club" and it's such a great way to grow up. I have many fun times to share with you and if you're anywhere near as horse mad as me, I'm sure you'll enjoy reading this book.

Now, from the beginning...

Monday 24 September

When I heard Sparkle nicker this morning, I knew she was calling me. I raced over to the paddock still in my PJs. I couldn't get there quickly enough! I can't believe I now actually have my own pony! And she's such a beautiful palomino. They've always been my favorite type of horse and now I have one of my very own. It's like a dream come true. One minute, I'm being led around the paddock on my neighbor's horse and the next minute I'm standing there with my own palomino.

I'm lucky as well, to have a girl like Ali as my neighbor. She's really nice to me and also a great rider. If it wasn't for her living next door with horses of her own, this probably wouldn't be happening. She and her mum know everything there is to know about horses, which is such a great help, because my parents don't know much at all. And now that I have my own pony to ride, we can go riding together. It's great having an older girl next door who is as horse mad as me. I always wanted a big sister. I'm very lucky!

And guess what! Sparkle loves bananas. Who would ever have thought that horses would eat bananas – with the skin and all! I'm going to give her one every day as a special treat. I'll have to make sure Mom buys lots of carrots as well. I'm so glad it's the school holidays and I can spend every day with her. My new grooming kit is really cool too – it's in a special pink box and everything in it is pink. And the best part is…Sparkle loves being brushed. She's such a good pony and Ali says I'm very lucky to have found a pony with a quiet temperament like hers.

I can't wait for my first riding lesson on Thursday. The instructor is coming at 9:00 in the morning before it gets hot, so I'll have to be up early to make sure I'm ready. I don't think I'll be able to sleep tonight, just thinking about it! I'm so excited!!!

Thursday 27 September

I thought that the day Sparkle arrived at our place was the best day of my life, but I think today was even better. That riding lesson was so awesome and Jane, the instructor, says I'm a natural. She said I have a really good seat and Mom was commenting on my posture and how straight I sit in the saddle. I just have to work on pulling Sparkle up when I want her to slow down. Even though she's 16 years old, she's very forward moving. But that's why she's such a good sporting pony and I can't wait to see Josh ride her in the gymkhana on Sunday.

He was really sad to sell her, but she's too small for him now. His new horse Tara, is beautiful, but Josh says that Sparkle is the best sporting pony and he's really keen to do well in the gymkhana. Anyway, I agreed to let him take her this Sunday so he can compete on her one last time. I can't wait to go and watch! I've never been to a gymkhana before; it's going to be so much fun.

And Ali said that we could go riding together tomorrow. That will be cool. She'll be able to give me a lesson and help me improve my riding. Mom said I can only ride in the small paddock though, until Sparkle and I get used to each other.

Ali and I are becoming really close; I think she's my best friend now. And it's fun sitting in our special tree. That's what we've decided to do now when we finish riding each day - take some snacks, climb up and sit in our special tree in the big paddock and just watch the horses grazing. Mom says I now have my very own saddle club. That's my favorite TV show but I never thought I'd have a saddle club of my own. IT'S TOTALLY COOL!

Sunday 29 September

Oh my gosh, today was AMAZING!!! Sparkle won 4 blue ribbons, 2 red and one green and Josh gave them all to me. I'm so happy!

Sparkle is the best sporting pony, I can't wait to do gymkhanas on her myself. That bounce pony looks like so much fun and Sparkle is really good at it. And she's so good at barrels as well. But the jumping was the best – Sparkle is such a good all-rounder! Of course, Josh is a really good rider and really pushed her on, but I know I'll be able to do that too. Especially on Sparkle. What a talented pony!

And she looked so pretty today. I spent all yesterday afternoon getting her ready. It was so much fun in the paddock with Ali. We bathed her with this special horsey shampoo that made her coat look really shiny and Ali showed me how to braid her mane and tail as well. It looked very professional, especially with the colored ribbon that we braided through it. And the brow band that Josh's Mom made for her looked terrific. She said that I can keep it and she's even going to make me another one with ribbon the colors of my pony club, when I eventually join.

I can't wait till school goes back and I can tell all my friends about her – they'll be so jealous! I wonder if I'd be able to take her to school for show and tell? Miss Johnson might let me!

Tuesday 2 October

I can't believe it! Cammie and Grace now have a horse too. They're the girls who moved in across the road recently and with all 4 of us, we can have a proper saddle club. Four girls in the one street all with horses. They have to share Rocket – that's the name of their new horse (apparently he's really fast).

We're planning to meet up in the big paddock tomorrow. They don't have anywhere to keep Rocket but Ali's mum said it's fine for him to stay in their paddock for the time being. We'll all be able to go riding together. Their dad knows heaps about horses as well. He grew up on a horse property, so I guess he'll teach them how to ride.

I'm having another riding lesson with Jane tomorrow. This time I'm going to work on my rising trot. Ali's been teaching me how to do it properly already, so I bet Jane will be surprised at how good I am.

Sparkle loves the new hay that we've bought – it's top quality grass hay and as soon as she sees me with it, she comes cantering over. She's such a beautiful pony, the other girls all think so as well. I'm so lucky to have a palomino – she's definitely the prettiest horse!

Friday 5 October

IT'S NOT FAIR! Ali is MY friend and the tree in the big paddock is OUR special tree! Now Cammie has come along and taken Ali off me. They spent the whole afternoon together in the paddock with the horses and Ali showed Cammie our tree. That's where I found them when I finally got home today after going to the saddlery with Mom. She bought me a brand new pink feed bucket that is really cool. I was so happy because I found lots of things that I'd like for my birthday as well. It's only a month away and Mom said that she'd think about them. Hopefully she'll go back and buy them for me. Anyway, I raced over to the paddock to show Sparkle and give her a banana and there they were…both Ali and Cammie up in our tree together. And the worst part was that they weren't even interested in me. It's probably because they're the same age and I'm younger but it's not fair – Ali is MY special friend!

Mom said that we'll all have to just get along and that I can spend time with Grace, who is more my age. But I'm really upset about Ali. I can see that she and Cammie are going to become best friends now. I liked it when it was just the two of us. Why did the other girls have to come along and spoil it all?

Sunday 7 October

It was really scary today! My friend Ella came over with her brother Tim just as I was getting ready to go for a ride. Anyway, Mom said they could come to the paddock with us to have a little ride themselves. They were so excited as neither of them had ever been on a horse before.

Mom put the saddle on while I did up the bridle (Mom still can't figure out how to put it on properly). We led Ella around the paddock first. She was having such a great time. Then Tim decided that he wanted a turn. To make it a bit more exciting, Mom got Sparkle to trot while she was leading her. But then all of a sudden she turned Sparkle to the left. It was a really sharp turn. Sparkle was fine but it made the saddle slip completely down to her side. She just kept trotting along, not worried in the slightest, but Tim was almost on the ground.

Mom hadn't done the girth up tightly enough! She should know by now that it gets loose after a few minutes of riding. We all thought it looked so funny with Tim hanging on like that. Sparkle wasn't going very fast and he was hanging on really tightly so he was actually okay. But he didn't think so! It scared him half to death. He was even shaking. I'd forgotten it was his first ride on a horse – EVER – and he just isn't used to it. I hope this doesn't put him off riding.

But it was what happened next that scared EVERYBODY! Someone must have left the gate open because Rocket had wandered into Sparkle's paddock. When he saw us all gathered around Tim and Sparkle, he got all stirred up and galloped over. All of a sudden, he did a huge kick and came SO close to kicking Ella in the head. His hooves looked like they just missed her!

She screamed and this made him go even crazier. I think it

was the scariest thing I've ever seen! Just before that, all of us were laughing at Tim. Watching him slide down Sparkle's side while she trotted along looked pretty funny. But then in the blink of an eye Ella was almost being kicked in the head by a huge horse. Mom was still freaking out about it after dinner tonight – she said she can't stop thinking about what could have happened. I don't think she'll ever forget to tighten the girth again, that's for sure!

Actually, I don't think any of us will ever forget what happened today!

And now I have to go back to school tomorrow. At least I can see all my friends and tell them about Sparkle. (I don't want to tell them about the near accident though – they mightn't want to come over if I do).

As soon as I get home, I'm going to race over to the paddock and give Sparkle a banana. I hope we have some. I'd better go and check – if there's none maybe Mom can get some more on her way home from work.

Monday 8 October

School was so boring today. I just wanted to come home to Sparkle. All I could think about was my baby. I told all my friends about her and they're so jealous! They all wish that they had a horse. Everyone wants to come over and have a ride. Mom said, maybe not just yet. She's still getting over what happened yesterday. At least Ella is okay – and Tim as well. Ella and I were laughing about what happened to him. That was the funniest thing. But he doesn't think so.

Sparkle loved her banana this afternoon. I didn't ride, I just patted her and watched her grazing. She's the prettiest horse! I could see Ali and Cammie with their horses over at Ali's place. They waved to me but didn't come over.

I knew they'd become best friends. I don't know where Grace was.

At least I have my baby – Sparkle…AND my darling cat Soxy – I know that THEY love me!!!!

Wednesday 10 October

Dad put an ad in the paper to see if we can agist our big paddock. If we can get someone to keep their horse here, the money will help to pay for Sparkle's feed and my riding lessons. And just tonight a lady rang. She's coming over tomorrow to have a look. Dad said that she has a daughter who needs somewhere to keep her horse. She has a friend with another 2 horses as well and she doesn't have anywhere to keep them either. The lady told Dad that the girls are both good riders. They're about 4 years older than me but he said she sounded very nice and he thinks this could work out really well. Maybe the girls will be able to help me with my riding? Maybe we'll even become good friends! That would be cool, especially now that Ali is spending all her time with Cammie and Grace. It will be so good to have some other horsey friends of my own.

I hope they're friendly and that they do decide to keep their horses here. I can't wait to meet them tomorrow. I wonder what their horses are like? I hope they get along with Sparkle!

Thursday 11 October

Shelley and Kate are super nice and their horses are gorgeous. They love our place and think it'll be perfect. This is going to be so cool. If I introduce them to Cammie, Grace and Ali, they might even be happy to include me again and that means we can have a real saddle club – there'll be so many of us. I just wish we had proper stables like in the Saddle Club TV show. That would be really cool. But instead, we have to cross over our creek to get to the horse paddocks and it's so far to walk, especially carrying all the tack. I'm glad Mom carries the saddle for me!

Shelley and Kate are going to bring their horses to our place on Saturday and we've planned to go riding together. This is so exciting, I can't wait! And they've even said that they'll pay me to feed their horses each day. That's so good because now I'll be able to save up and buy those really pretty jodhpurs that I saw at Saddle World last weekend. Mom said I'm going to have to get up even earlier in the mornings now, so that I'm ready for school on time. But I don't mind.

Saturday 13 October

Our place is just like the Saddle Club now! Shelley and Kate brought their horses over today and we all went riding together. Then we spent the afternoon bathing and grooming them. It's so much fun having girls at my house and doing all this horsey stuff together. It's way better than having to do it on my own. Mom says the problem with Cammie and Grace is that they're keeping their horses at Ali's and that's why they've become best friends. But I have my own special horsey friends now. And they're keeping their horses at my house.

This afternoon we all just got to hang out and talk about horses. Shelley has a bay and Kate has a chestnut. The other horse is a paint and he belongs to Kate as well, but she doesn't ride him much. Sparkle seems to get along with them all so that's really good. And now she has lots of horses in the paddocks around hers so she definitely won't get lonely.

We met Kate's dad today when he brought the horses over and he told us that we could borrow his horse trailer anytime. This means I might be able to go to pony club when it starts up again next year. Shelley and Kate have told me all about it and it sounds amazing! I can't wait for that!

Sunday 14 October

A sound like thunder woke me up at 5:30 this morning. At first I couldn't work out what it was because I was still half asleep. But then I realized it was horses' hooves galloping past my bedroom window. I heard Mom and Dad running down the stairs so I jumped out of bed and ran up the driveway after them.

Shelley and Kate's horses had escaped from the paddock and ran down the hill and across the creek. There's not much water in it at the moment and it's easy to cross. They must have been trying to get out the front gate but luckily they found the big feed bins that we keep in the shed. At least that stopped them from going out onto the road! We found them up there stuffing themselves with whatever they could find. Luckily it was only chaff but Mom and Dad were in a panic. The horses were really excited and stirring each other up, especially Nugget. He's the paint and he seemed to be the ringleader.

Mom, Dad and I were all running around in our PJs, with lead ropes and some hay, trying to catch them all. Mom and Dad were NOT impressed - especially at 5:30 in the morning! It was so hard to catch them and calm them down. Luckily there were 3 of us – It took quite a while to get them under control and back in their paddock. Dad then had to fix the gate.

What a way to start the day!

Dad rang Tom (Kate's dad) and he said that Nugget is an escape artist. When Shelley and Kate came over this afternoon, they said that he's escaped from a lot of paddocks. Dad was annoyed because Tom hadn't told us that before. He's going to try to find somewhere else to keep Nugget now. This will be good because we don't want that happening again!

At least we all got to go for a ride. When we went over to the paddock, Ali, Cammie and Grace were riding at Ali's. Our paddock is the best one for riding in though because it's so big. I introduced them to Shelley and Kate and asked them if they wanted to ride with us. Ali, Cammie and Grace were SO nice to me. I could see that they really wanted to be friends with the older girls as well. But Cammie's probably a bit jealous – I know that she wants to keep Ali to herself.

It was heaps of fun with us all riding together though and hopefully now we can all meet up after school one day this week and go riding again – that will be awesome if we do!

I hope the girls get on okay. It'd be great if we can all become good friends!

Kate's paint - Nugget

The Escape Artitst!!!

Monday 15 October

When I got home from school today, I found that Nugget was missing from the paddock. I was so worried because I thought he'd escaped again but then Dad told me they've found somewhere else to keep him. Dad was really relieved and said it would be less to worry about. It's also one less horse for me to have to feed each morning and night. But that means less money as well and that's not good because I really want to be able to buy those jodhpurs as soon as I can.

I'm really excited though because Tom, Kate's Dad, brought a heap of horse jumps over and put them in the paddock. Kate's horse Lulu is a really good jumper and Kate loves jumping so she wants to practice. Tom said that he'd teach me how to jump on Sparkle as well. This is very exciting – I really want to learn how to jump – it looks like so much fun. It'll probably be scary at first but Tom said I can just go over little jumps until I become confident. I know that Sparkle is a good jumper as well, so I'm sure she'll love it too. This is so cool!!!

Wednesday 17 October

I had a great time this afternoon. There were actually all 6 of us riding in the paddock together and everyone was so friendly to each other. I was really worried about that, especially with Cammie and I didn't know how it would work out. But even though we're all different ages, we get on really well. Shelley is the oldest – she's 13, Kate and Ali are both 12, Cammie is 11 and Grace and I are both 9. (Well, I'll turn 9 in just over three weeks' time – and I can't wait)!

And I got to try jumping!!! Kate and Shelley were telling me what to do. They were only small jumps but I loved it and so did Sparkle. Her ears went forward and she didn't even hesitate. I love her so much!

I saw a beautiful Wintec saddle at the saddlery on the weekend as well and I really hope that Mom and Dad buy it for my birthday present. It'll be so much easier to jump in than the Western saddle I'm using now. Ali's mom said I could borrow that until I get my own saddle. It's a great one to learn in because it helps hold me in place and I have less chance of falling off. But it's hard to rise up properly when I go for a jump.

The new Wintecs are so pretty and Shelley has one. She says it's fantastic. I'd really like to get some chaps of my own as well. Ali has loaned me her old pair but she has new ones and they look so cool. I should have enough money soon, but I want to get those jodhpurs as well – there are so many things I want to buy. Maybe I should just put them on my Christmas list?

I wonder if I'll get a new saddle for my birthday? I hope so! I can't wait!!!

Saturday 20 October

Mom was the only one at home today but it was lucky that she was there. Kate was trotting Lulu down the hill so she could hose her down after riding but her hoof got caught in some wire fencing. It's part of a gate that Dad made and someone left it lying across the track. Kate said that Lulu panicked and got all tangled up in it. Kate fell off her and it was so lucky that she wasn't hurt but Lulu's legs were all cut to pieces.

Shelley ran down to the house to get Mom and they managed to untangle Lulu. But her legs were really badly cut and Mom had to call the vet. Thank goodness Lulu's going to be okay! Kate's not going to be able to ride her until she heals though and that could take a couple of weeks! Kate was really upset and rang her Dad. She said he got really angry and wants to talk to us about paying the vet bill.

Now Mom and Dad are upset – they don't want to have to pay someone else's vet bill! I don't know what's going to happen. I hope that the girls can still stay here. It's been so much better since they arrived - the others are so much nicer to me now and we're all able to ride together. It has to work out.

Monday 22 October

We had visitors this afternoon and they left the front gate open! I'd brought Sparkle down to graze on the nice grass around the house and when I went to check on her, I couldn't find her anywhere. I just knew that she'd probably walked up the driveway and out the gate.

Mom and I raced down the street looking for her. We were so worried that she might have wandered down towards the main road. We couldn't see her anywhere so we headed up to the horsey property at the end of our street in case she'd gone there but no one had seen her.

We had to look down every driveway and Mom was getting really stressed. Then we walked up Cammie and Grace's driveway and that was like climbing a mountain, it's so steep. It was the only place we hadn't been to though. Then all of a sudden we spotted her in amongst some bushes. But as soon as she saw us, she decided to bolt. I didn't think we were going to be able to catch her at all but luckily I took a banana with me. She just couldn't resist! Then we managed to get the halter and lead rope on her and walk her home.

I'm so glad we found her – I don't know what I would have done if she'd gone missing! We're going to have to put a sign on the gate so people close it when they come in, in future.

Mom and Dad can't believe so many things have gone wrong since Sparkle arrived. At least it's all sorted out with Kate's dad now. He came over and worked out the vet bill with Dad. He's blaming us for the wire gate that was lying across the track. We don't know whose fault that was but Dad's just going to give him free agistment for a couple of weeks. Anyway, he's happy with that. And thank goodness Lulu is going to be okay. She just has to rest for another 10 days or so and then Kate should be able to ride her again. I'm so pleased about that and so is Kate. It would be terrible to have a horse and not be able to ride her!

My baby. I'm so glad she's safe!!!

Wednesday 7 November

I just haven't had a chance to write lately – I've been so busy looking after all the horses - especially now that the girls want me to rug them. This keeps their coats looking nice and stops them from getting bitten. I really need to get a summer rug for Sparkle as well. It's so much extra work putting the rugs on and off, but at least the summer ones can stay on all day. They actually protect the horses and help to keep them cool. I didn't know that! I'll definitely have to get one for my baby!

I'm SO excited because this Sunday is my birthday!!! – Finally! And all my friends are coming over for a pool party sleepover on Saturday. I can't wait to show them Sparkle. Mom said that we'll be able to give them pony rides on the grass by the pool. She said that she'll put Sparkle on a lead rope and lead them around. I can't wait!

I wonder if I'll get that new saddle? Mom and Dad said they won't tell me what they've got for me. They said it's a surprise and I have to wait. I hope it's the Wintec! I'm so excited – I'm definitely not going to be able to sleep tonight.

Sunday 11 November

It was the BEST BIRTHDAY EVER!!!!!

My party was amazing! Everyone arrived yesterday afternoon and the first thing they wanted to do was see Sparkle – they think she's so pretty and they all wanted to pat and brush her. I think she loved the attention. They all loved riding her as well. Mom and I led them around on the lead rope. Of course we made sure that the girth was extra tight and everyone was safe. Most of them live in suburban houses and don't get to be on a property so they always enjoy coming to my house. It's so much better now that I have a horse though!

And Nate even gave them rides on his motorbike. He can be the best brother when he wants to be! I think he was proud to show off his new bike and was more than happy to give all my friends a double around our house. That's another great thing about Sparkle, she's totally bomb proof and doesn't get scared of anything really. Her last owner Josh, rode motorbikes too, so I guess she's become used to them. This is great because it doesn't bother her at all when Nate and his friends ride their bikes in the paddock near hers.

My party ended up being heaps of fun – we spent hours in the pool, jumping off our diving deck. It's the best thing and we were all lining up in a row, holding hands and jumping in together. Mom took some great action photos as well with us in mid-air – they're so cool! The trampoline by the pool is heaps of fun as well and everyone just loved it. Dad set up lights around the pool area and also a mirror ball in the gazebo with lots of black plastic for the lights to shine on. We had flame torches lit in the garden as well and it was so beautiful once it got dark. Everyone was commenting on how pretty it looked.

After dinner, we had a disco in the gazebo and the mirror ball and all the lights looked awesome. Everyone thinks I'm so lucky that my dad is a musician because he set up his big speakers for us and even some microphones with stands for us to sing. We had the music really loud and everyone was dancing and singing and having so much fun. We played really cool games as well like Freeze, where you have to stand still when the music stops and also the limbo.

Mom and Dad had set up our big family tent down on the grass and we all slept in there. What a great night – a bit squashy but we all managed to fit. Ali, Cammie, Grace and I talked about horsey stuff all night. We hardly got any sleep. I'm so glad they came – we're getting on really well now and Grace and I are becoming great friends. It's probably because we're more the same age. Everyone else was telling us to be quiet because they wanted to go to sleep. I guess we all eventually drifted off, but I'm sure it was really late when we did.

Then today, we spent pretty much the whole day in the pool – and singing on the microphones as well. Tina, my best friend from school wouldn't stop. Dad said that you could hear her all the way down our driveway and we're sure our neighbors were glad when she finally went home. I think she wants to be a rock star when she gets older. Hopefully her voice improves!

And then late this afternoon after everyone left, Mom and Dad gave me my present. And it's the WINTEC!! They wanted to wait until everyone had gone so we could have some special family time together. Oh my gosh, I was so excited when I saw what it was. It looks so shiny and new – especially after riding the old western style saddle that Ali's Mom has been lending me. I was so used to that.

I'm really going to look after my new saddle. It comes in a

special protective bag that I can keep it in when I'm not riding. Mom said that Sparkle and I won't know ourselves – I'm sure that she's going to find it much more comfortable as well.

I can't wait to go riding tomorrow and show the girls. As soon as I get home from school I'm going to race over to the paddock and go for a ride.

I'm so lucky – it was the best birthday ever!!!

Tina being a rock star!!! Ha Ha Ha!

Monday 12 November

Just when everything seemed to be going well…

I found a huge cut and a bruise in the shape of a hoof on Sparkle's side. Shelly's horse, Millie has become the boss of the paddock and I'm sure she must have kicked Sparkle. Millie's such a bossy horse and so greedy at feed times. Even though she has food in her own feed bin, she wants Sparkle's as well. She races across the paddock with her ears back and kicks out at Sparkle so she can get her food. Then she races back to her own feed bin to eat that too! She's so greedy! And it's so hard to make sure each horse gets their share when Millie's in the paddock. I think I'm going to have to take Sparkle out and feed her on her own in future.

And now I can't even use my new Wintec because the cut on her side is right in the saddle area. So it'll hurt her too much to have a saddle on. I wonder how long it'll take for the cut to heal? Not too long I hope! I can't believe I won't be able to ride her and just when I have a brand new saddle as well. But Mom said…you get what you focus on! She's always saying that and the strange thing is, she's usually right. So now I'm going to focus on Sparkle getting better quickly so I can use the Wintec and take her for a ride. I bet she'll love the new saddle just as much as me.

I'm going to ask Mom and Dad if I can take the Wintec to school for show and tell – that would be really cool. I'm sure Miss Johnson won't mind. I think I'll ask her tomorrow.

Thursday 15 November

Mom and Dad took me to school today with my new saddle so I could show my class. They really liked it and I had to tell everyone the names of all the parts and how to adjust the stirrups and all. A lot of the kids have never even ridden a horse before so they knew nothing about it. Miss Johnson's such an animal lover, she was really interested as well. She brings her dog to school sometimes. She's a really cute Bassett Hound, called Shelby. Miss Johnson isn't married and doesn't have any kids so Shelby's like her baby. She's such a well-behaved dog and we're allowed to pat her and play with her. She sits right beside Miss Johnson's desk while we're in class – she's so cute! Miss Johnson said that she'll take photos of each of us with Santa hats on holding Shelby and we can use the photos to make Christmas cards.

And also, the BEST news is that Miss Johnson said I can bring Sparkle to school one day next week. Dad said that he would bring her in Tom's trailer and Miss Johnson said he can drive the trailer straight onto the oval. Then we can unload her right there and the whole class can go and look at her. How awesome is that!!! Everyone is so excited! She's such a quiet pony and she loves people, so she'll be fine, I know it. They'll have to keep their distance though. Miss Johnson said we all have to stay safe and no one will be able to get close to her or pat her or anything, but that's okay. It'll just be great to show her to everyone. This is the best thing ever. I bet nobody has ever taken a pony to school for show and tell – not at my school anyway!

I can't wait for next week!

Saturday 17 November

Sparkle's cut has nearly healed but Jim (Cammie and Grace's Dad), said I should wait a few more days before I ride her. It wouldn't be fair to put a saddle on top of that cut – it would hurt her too much and probably make it bleed again, so I just have to wait. It was still fun though because Grace and I were watching the other girls practice their jumping today and we were able to reset the jumps for them when they knocked them down. It was so great watching Kate jump Lulu. Her legs have completely healed and she was flying over the jumps. She can jump over 3 feet – that is so high! I can't wait until I can do that on Sparkle!

Grace and Cammie are still sharing their horse, Rocket and Grace said that because I couldn't ride Sparkle, then she wouldn't ride today either. So we just hung around together in the paddock and had fun. We're becoming such good friends now – we get along really well. She came over and swam in the pool with me this afternoon as well – that was great fun too. I love having a best friend as a neighbor. I'm so lucky.

There are no boys in our street for Nate to play with though, just heaps of girls – and we're all horse mad! He gets annoyed about that and says it isn't fair – but Dad takes him surfing all the time and he goes off motorbike riding with his friends, so he still gets to have fun. Mom says that we're both so lucky to have a property where we can ride horses AND motor bikes.

Nate has tried riding Sparkle and he even had a lesson with Jane, the instructor. But he doesn't like horse riding much. He says that he feels much safer on his motorbike. Mom said it's because he has control of his bike but doesn't feel the same when he's on a horse. I think that motorbikes are scary to ride – not horses! It's okay when he doubles me, but I still get scared. I did try having a go on my own a couple of times and Dad said I just have to practice so I'm more confident. I might try it again – Nate loves it when I ride his bike. But I definitely prefer horses!

We got a great surprise today as well because Tom put some barrels in the paddock so we can practice barrel racing. He brought logs as well and said we can put the logs on the barrels to make more jumps. So now we'll be able to set up a proper jumping course. Ali said we should paint colored stripes on them. I asked Dad and he found some leftover paint in our shed for us to use. He repainted our house last year, so we have heaps of leftover paint and brushes. It was really fun and the barrels and logs look so good – some have blue and white stripes and some have pink and white (the pink was leftover from painting my bedroom).

Ali is really arty. She's so clever and has such great ideas. It was so much fun painting all the equipment together. She also said we should use the spare logs for bounce pony. And we even made some bending poles. Dad found some special thin poles that are perfect and he mixed up cement to put into ice cream containers so we could stand the poles in them.

Now there's so much for us to do rather than just ride around the paddocks. I can't wait to join pony club next year so I can go to gymkhanas and do all of the events. Kate and Shelley have competed in heaps of them and won so many medals and ribbons. I know that Sparkle is a really good sporting pony and she already knows how to do all of these things. As soon as I can ride her again, I'm going to practice on her.

Sunday 18 November

We all met in the paddock again today and set up the jumps. The paint was dry so we could move the barrels and logs around. It looks so cool and now we have our own jumping course. The girls came up with the BEST idea as well. We're going to have our own gymkhana right here in our paddock. We can organize all the events and do jumping, barrels, bounce pony and bending. Ali's going to make some ribbons for the winners and we're going to ask all the parents to come and watch. Kate and Shelley are going to work out a program and get it all typed up so it's really official.

This will be so cool and Mom and Dad think it's a great idea as well. I can't wait!

Shelley with Millie

Tuesday 20 November

Finally, Sparkle's cut has healed and I was able to ride her today. The Wintec is so awesome! It's so comfortable and Sparkle looks perfect with it on her back. It's so much nicer than the shabby old western saddle I was using. Mom says I have to be very grateful that Ali's mom loaned it to me though. And I really am! I think I'll make her a thank you card and take it over to her tomorrow. I think she'll like that.

The Wintec is so much easier to jump in as well. And today I even managed a 2 foot high jump. I'm so proud of myself and of Sparkle too. She's such a good pony and I love watching her ears go forward when she goes over the jumps. I think she loves jumping just as much as me! I have to practice keeping my eyes straight ahead though, facing in the direction that I want her to go. Ali was in the paddock this afternoon helping me – it's so good to have someone telling me what I'm doing wrong. Mom said that I'll learn so much quicker this way. Mom always picks up the jumps if Sparkle knocks any down. She's always in the paddock with me when I ride. She helps me to tack up and tightens the girth when it gets loose. (She'll never forget that again!)

I had the best ride today! After jumping I had a go at barrels, bending and even bounce pony. Sparkle knows exactly what to do. I just have to push her on using my leg aids. She's pretty fast and I'm becoming so much more confident.

I'm going to keep practicing every afternoon if I can, so I'll be ready for our gymkhana. We'll probably have it in a couple of weeks. We have to work out a day when all the girls and the parents are free. Hopefully we'll be able to have it soon.

Oh and the best news as well – Miss Johnson told me today that I can bring Sparkle to school any day this week. I just have to check when Dad can get some time off work to take her. This is so exciting! I can't believe I'll get to take my pony to school for show and tell!

I love jumping!

Thursday 22 November

Oh my gosh!!! Today was incredible. Dad brought Sparkle to school in the horse trailer. It was during the morning session before the morning tea play break. He drove the trailer onto the oval and unloaded her right there. My whole class went down to look at her but Miss Johnson made everyone stand right back, just to be safe.

She asked me to demonstrate how to groom and brush her and how to clean her hooves with the hoof pick. Dad held her lead rope and she just stood there so quietly the whole time. Then Miss Johnson just couldn't resist – she had to go and pat her and she thought she was beautiful. She even gave her a hug.

Then all the kids wanted to pat her too and Miss Johnson said it was okay because she could see how quiet Sparkle is. They all had turns patting her and she just stood there so quietly the whole time. Everyone adored her – she's so well-behaved. Miss Johnson was raving about how beautiful she is and I felt so proud!

Everyone said that it was the best show and tell they've ever seen. And so did Miss Johnson. I'm so lucky to have her for a teacher. And I'm so lucky to have Sparkle for a pony.

Tuesday 11 December

I can't believe it's been almost 3 whole weeks since I've had a chance to write! I never seem to get much time for my diary lately - things have been so hectic lately, especially with all the horses.

Grace now has her own pony – a beautiful 14 hand chestnut called, Trixie. So now she won't have to share Rocket with Cammie. They'll each have their own pony and this is perfect for our gymkhana. We've decided to have it on the Saturday after Christmas because everyone's busy until then.

I can't believe that Christmas is only 14 days away and the school holidays are almost here! In 3 days I'll have 6 weeks off school and I'll be able to spend every day with Sparkle. The girls and I are so excited. We have so much planned! We're going to have sleep-overs at each other's houses and go riding EVERY day. We'll have to get up really early to ride though because it's SO hot now. Yesterday was almost 100 degrees and way too hot for riding! But the early mornings are perfect and so are the late afternoons when it cools down. I think that's my favorite time. It's so good in summer because it gets dark so much later and we now have more time in the afternoons to ride.

I'm so glad we have a pool! It's so hot, we'll be able to go swimming every day. And Grace and Cammie are getting a pool put in too. They're hoping it'll be ready for Christmas.

And the best news is, they're now going to keep their two horses in our front paddock rather than at Ali's. Our front paddock is right across the road from their driveway and it's much quicker and easier for them to feed and look after their horses. So Dad is going to buy a heap of special wire and posts to fence the paddock for them. The money that Jim pays Dad for keeping Rocket and Trixie will help to pay for Sparkle. We've started giving her special food and it's really expensive. But she seems to be getting skinny and we don't know why. We're hoping that the new food will fatten her up and make her really healthy. I'm so happy because the girls will be at my house all the time now, instead of always being at Ali's. This is going to be so cool!

I can't wait for Christmas. My list this year is full of horsey stuff. I might even get those jodhpurs that I've been wanting. They're so expensive, I still haven't saved up enough to buy them myself. Luckily Ali has given me her old ones to wear and Mom even found some blue ones at the 2nd hand shop that almost look brand new. And they fit me perfectly! I'd love to have the brand new pair that I saw at Saddle World though. I know they still have them because I saw them when I was in there with Grace the other day. Maybe Santa will give them to me?

I can't wait!

Grace's new pony, Trixie. So pretty!

Tuesday 25 Dec

We had an awesome Christmas Day!

Nate and I got up at 5am and ran in to wake up Mom and Dad. But we had to wait for Nana to get up and make a cup of tea before we could start opening our presents. She always takes so long! She arrived a few days ago and she's staying for 2 weeks. I was really excited because I thought that she could come to the gymkhana, but Mom said that she probably won't be able to make it across our creek. She's pretty wobbly when she walks and needs some help. Mom said that she'll have to get her a special walker soon so that she can get around easily.

I got the best presents and Santa gave me the jodhpurs I wanted. They're exactly the same as the ones in Saddle World and they look so cool. I tried them on and they fit perfectly. I'm so glad that he got the size right!

I got a new pair of chaps as well – they're the same as Ali's. I've been wanting some like hers for ages. As well as that I got some new riding boots. Now I don't have to wear Ali's hand me downs - but Mom said that I should still keep them as a spare pair. It's always good to have a pair to lend to friends when they come over for a ride, so they'll be perfect for that.

I got a brand new grooming kit as well. Sparkle stepped on my old one and the case is all broken, so now I'll have lots of brushes. When my friends come over there'll be plenty of brushes to groom Sparkle with. I also got a new purple lead rope. I've just been using a faded old green one that Josh's mom gave me when we brought Sparkle home. This one will look so much better!

I LOVE SPARKLE!!

It's funny because I got pretty much all horsey stuff and Nate got things for motorbike riding. He also got a drum kit. Mom says that he's spoilt but Dad says that it's fair because I have Sparkle. Dad wants us all to be musicians and play instruments like him. Nate is really good on the guitar and I guess now, he'll have to learn the drums as well. He's so excited about it. At least he can play them in Dad's music room up at our shed. Lucky it's sound proof!

I made Sparkle a special mash for her Christmas breakfast. I chopped up apples and carrots and added her favorite – some mashed banana. Then I mixed it with oats and chaff and added some of her favorite grass hay. She thought it was delicious! You should have seen her licking her lips. It was so cute! She kept dropping bits on the ground but that made Sheba happy. I think she enjoyed it as much as Sparkle! Sheba's our golden retriever and she ÁLWAYS comes over to the paddock with me when I go to ride or feed Sparkle. She loves it and always has her nose in a bush somewhere. All we can see is her backside and tail poking out and her tail is always wagging. She's so happy just sniffing around looking to see what she can find. She's great in the paddock too and loves wandering around when I'm riding. The horses are used to her and don't mind her at all.

It's so funny because my cat Soxy - who is the most adorable ginger cat you've ever seen - has started coming over to the paddock with us. Mom says it looks hilarious. There's me, Sheba and Soxy all walking together. I would have thought a cat would be scared of horses but Soxy loves it over there. When we get to the creek though, I have to carry him. He just sits there looking at me and waiting to be picked up. The creek is really low at the moment because we haven't had rain for ages. So he can jump across without getting wet. When there's more water in it though, I have to carefully cross by jumping from one big rock to another. Dad's going to get a proper crossing made soon. That'll be so much better. He's just worried about it getting washed away if the creek floods. This happens when there's lots of rain, but hopefully he'll be able to work something out.

I had the best Christmas! Mom, Dad, Nate and Nana loved the presents I gave them as well. It was great this year because I saved enough money from feeding all the horses and I could buy really good presents for everyone.

Now we've got the gymkhana to look forward to! We're going to have it next Saturday afternoon and that's actually New Year's Eve. The girls are all really excited and so am I!

I LOVE CHRISTMAS!

Tuesday 1 January

New Year's Day!

Yesterday we finally got to have our gymkhana. We spent all morning getting ready and we were so excited! The girls and I set up a really cool jumping course, the bending poles and also bounce pony. The paddock looked so good with all the colored stripes that we painted on the equipment. And we were so glad that the weather was fine! We were really worried because there's a cyclone up north and the weatherman said that heavy rain and flooding is on the way. But there was no sign of it at our place, just more beaming sunshine.

The parents started arriving at 3:00 in the afternoon. They all brought fold up chairs and we set them up under the shade of some trees. So they had a really good spot to sit. Dad even drove Nana around to Ali's place and set up a comfy chair for her in the shade so she could watch the gymkhana from there. They all brought some drinks and snacks and said they were getting ready to celebrate New Year's Eve.

It all started off really well. We each did the jumping course a couple of times. In the end we decided not to score each other, but just have fun. Tom was helping us all with our jumping and pretty much giving us each a jumping lesson as we went along. This was really cool because he knows a lot about jumping and was really helpful. Then everyone ended up getting a ribbon. Ali ended up making one for everyone!

Just as we were about to start the other events, we suddenly heard a scream. Cammie decided to take Rocket for a ride in the big paddock and for some reason, he bolted. Then almost in a flash I saw Cammie on the ground. She had fallen off Rocket and then he raced off up the hill. Everyone went running towards her in a panic – it was really scary!

I felt my heart stop and I couldn't move. I could see her lying on the ground but she was completely still. Her Dad bent over her and we just stood waiting – I was really hoping that she was okay. Then he moved away from her and she slowly stood up. She was shaken up and she was crying. I was praying that she wasn't hurt. We've heard terrible stories of people coming off horses and being badly injured and I didn't want that happening to Cammie.

She took her helmet off and sat down with all the parents. Tom then went to catch Rocket and we all rushed over to her – we were so worried, but thank goodness, she was fine. She told us to go on with the gymkhana, so we did but it kind of wasn't the same after that.

Then Shelley and Kate's parents said that they had to go and get ready for New Year's Eve. Cammie, Grace and Ali asked me if they could stay the night at my house. Their parents said that they might come over as well and have a barbecue with us. Mom and Dad said that this was a great idea.

The girls and I decided to set the tent up so we could camp out for the night, just like at my birthday party. So Dad helped us get organized and set up while Mom got the food ready. Thank goodness, Cammie wasn't hurt badly. She said that her wrist hurt a bit from the fall and she had some bruises on her hip, but that was all. She was so lucky!

I ended up having so much fun with the girls last night and Nate joined in as well. We had a nighttime swim in the pool and later on we all got torches and played spotlight. It gets so dark on our property at nighttime though and hiding in the bushes can get pretty scary. There was a lot of screaming going on, that's for sure! Then Mom and Dad gave us some sparklers and party poppers and we let them off right on midnight. We all counted down and then called out HAPPY NEW YEAR!!!!!

Finally we went to sleep in the tent. Mom and Dad had to get up during the night though because it started to rain and they wanted to check that we weren't getting wet. Then at about 6:00 this morning, Jim arrived to pick the girls up. That was so early for them to leave and the bad part was, I was left to clean up all the mess!

Now it's pouring with rain. Mom and Dad said that it's meant to get worse and there might even be flooding. I hope my baby is okay. I brought her down near the house this afternoon so she could graze on the nice grass. But there's thunder and lightning right now so I hope she's not getting spooked! I wish I had stables to keep her in, so she can stay nice and dry. I'm glad she now has a summer rug! That will help to protect her from some of the rain at least.

Oh no – the lights are flickering. This storm definitely seems to be getting worse. I hope we don't have a blackout! I don't think I'm going to be able to sleep tonight – I'm too worried about Sparkle! Maybe I should go and look for her and check that she's safe. I can't stop thinking about her. Is she going to be alright????

The rain won't stop! The creek is flooding!

I'm worried about Sparkle!!!

Find out what happens to Sparkle

in Book 2 of

Diary of a Horse Mad Girl…

Diary Of An Almost Cool Girl Book 1 - Meet Maddi…Ooops!

Dedication

Diary of an Almost Cool Girl is dedicated to the hundreds of "almost cool girls" I have taught over the years.
You are all very special! Don't ever let anyone tell you otherwise!
Thank you for giving me heaps of funny things to write about.

Where it all began...

The shrill sound of sirens vibrated the frame of the window I'm looking through. Up here on the second level of my school, I have a good view of the science block. Although the smoke haze is still lazily drifting from the windows that were smashed so the firemen could put their hoses in. Within a minute, they called out that the fire was under control.

I personally think the second fire unit and the two ambulances were a bit over the top. Nobody got hurt and the fire was only in the waste paper basket.

I've been sitting in the Principal's office now for about 15 minutes, waiting for my mom to arrive so that the Principal can inform her about, "How Madonna Bull tried to burn the school down."

They are his words – not mine.

How did I end up in the Principal's office, you ask. Well let me explain, it's all in my diary.

Monday

Hi everyone, welcome to my diary. Some people write their diaries as private memories for themselves, me…I'm different, I like to write it for an audience. My name is Madonna Bull, most people call me Maddi.

Some kids call me Mad or even Mad Bull, but I just ignore those types of kids. I'm not one of the "cool" kids and I'm not none of the "brainy" kids…I'm just a normal girl. Sometimes I like to think of myself as an "almost cool girl". Not in the "cool" group, but I'm not a nerd either.

I'm 12, well nearly 12. Okay, I'm 11 years, six months and 3 days to be exact.

I must confess, I have a bad habit. I like to give people nicknames, but don't panic, I don't call anyone by their nicknames, I just use them in my diary. So I guess only you and me know about them.

For example, my mom is an alternative hippy type mom, carefree and always looking on the bright side of things. Like when I dropped two dinner plates and they both broke, Mom just comes out with, "That's okay, Madonna, it just means less washing up to do."

And that is why her nickname is Mrs. Absolutely Positive. She is positive and enthusiastic about EVERYTHING! Mom also loves exercise, yoga and healthy food. She is really into those yucky green drinks with vegetables in them…gross!

Dad is big with a loud booming voice, so his nickname is Mr. Boom Boom. I wonder what my nickname for you would be if I knew you.

I blame my parents for the "nickname" thing. They give everyone in our neighborhood a nickname. Sometimes it is a bit embarrassing because we don't remember their real names. Labrador man (yes he walks a Labrador dog) and Bob (not his real name, but he is a builder – like in Bob the Builder) all live close by. So using nicknames is a family tradition that I have inherited.

My parents have given me some shocking nicknames. The first one was Poo Shooter because of my ability to shoot explosive poos across the room...when I was a baby.

When I got a bit older, around 6, they called me Princess Grotty Snotty, due to an unfortunate incident when I was wearing my best princess costume. I had a cold and my nose was full of thick gooey green snot.

Mom had taken me to the shopping center to go to the doctors and on the way out was taking a short cut through the food court. That's where it all went terribly wrong. Halfway through the eating area, a dear old granny type lady said to my mom, "What a beautiful princess you have there," – that's me of course. Granny lady stops eating her lovely looking cake and starts telling me how pretty I look. You know how, when you have a cold, you have no control over when your body decides to sneeze...well my body decided to sneeze just as she finished those kind words and smiled at me. Not just any sneeze, but perhaps the biggest and greatest sneeze in the history of mankind. Ahhhhh Chooooo!!!!

That stopped granny lady in her tracks. She looked down at her yummy cake and it is covered in two rivers of snot. She claps her hands across her mouth. Making retching sounds she races from her table towards the toilets. Meanwhile, mom grabs my hand and drags me off to the car. Being Mrs. Absolutely Positive she says, "It's okay, Maddi, better out than in. And besides, that cake was so unhealthy, she would have been much better off eating some nice fresh fruit." Did I mention that Mom is really into healthy food?

And that is how I collected the lovely nickname of Princess Grotty Snotty.

Anyway, enough diary for today. I need to do my homework and so probably do you.

Tuesday

My best friend Shelby and I walked to school this morning. We have been friends for a long time now, since about halfway through last year. I'm pretty quiet and try to avoid being the center of attention while Shelby is the opposite. She is loud and outgoing and loves being in the spotlight. Mom says we get along so well because we balance each other out. She said something about yin and yang, but I have no idea what she is talking about.

Today when we were in Music class we were sitting together as always. Mr. Canary (not his real name, just a great nickname, loves to sing his instructions to us), asked us to sit on the floor in a circle. Mr. Canary clapped out a rhythmic pattern and we each in turn had to copy his pattern. Of course the pattern changed for each student. Music is not my strong point, even when trying to clap the beat to a song, I'm likely to miss my own hands altogether. Obviously I'm not the only one feeling the pressure…as everyone is absolutely quiet as we await our turns.

There is a pause after each time Mr. Canary demonstrates a clapping pattern and in those few seconds you could hear a pin drop. It's nearly our turn, I can see Shelby is nervous as she keeps fidgeting. I'm so glad she is before me as it gives me a little more time. If you get the clapping pattern correct, Mr. Canary gives you a treat. So as well as not wanting to embarrass myself, I also really want a treat!

Mr. Canary claps out the rhythm for the girl sitting next to Shelby and the silence before the girl starts her turn seems absolute. Until an eardrum bursting fart noise rips across the room. I can even feel the vibration on the wooden floor and instantly realize that Shelby is the source of the noise. Poor Shelby! I feel embarrassed for her, so I try to think of something to say to ease her embarrassment.

No need – Shelby's next comment solves the problem. "Oh Maddi, that smells terrible!"

"I'm sorry Sir, Maddi has been suffering diarrhea, I'll just take her to the toilet and make sure she is okay." Then Shelby rustles me out of the classroom door as the laughter from the rest of the class drowns out my protests of innocence.

Once outside Shelby breaks into hysterical laughter, humiliating me even more.

But in the end I just give up and join in the laughter. Eventually Shelby says, "Well, Maddi, I may have ruined your image, but at least I got us out of clapping those stupid patterns."

Thursday

Despite the odd embarrassing moment, I'm lucky to have a good friend like Shelby. Having friends is especially important when you have a Bethany Barker in your class. Bethany is the mean girl of our school, some kids love sport, some love achieving A's, some love the arts, but Bethany just loves being mean. That's right folks, a genuine bully in my class.

Generally I don't have too much trouble with her. Shelby and I are nearly always together and Shelby is simply too loud to pick on. I've already told Bethany – whom I secretly call MG (short for mean girl) that I don't really care about her opinion.

One day MG must have been low on her quota of kids to pick on, when she came across Shelby and I in the playground. MG started making negative and nasty comments about my appearance. Like all bullies, MG always seemed to have a little band of followers. Sarah and Sue (who must be very desperate for friends to hand out with MG) were with MG. As usual, MG would make the nasty remarks and her followers, Sarah and Sue, would laugh at her "amazing" wit.

Mom always taught me the best way to deal with bullies is to ignore them or stand-up to them. I decided to try a bit of both. First I just totally ignored MG's nasty comments and I kept talking to Shelby.

After about 5 minutes of ignoring MG's little rant, I saw Shelby's face begin to show her anger at her friend being insulted. I put my hand softly on her shoulder and said, "It's okay, I'll handle this."

I turned to MG and calmly said, "Thanks Bethany, I'm always ready to accept constructive criticism about my appearance from intelligent, fashionable and thoughtful people like yourself."

Bethany looked confused.

Then I continued in a calm and confident voice, "But hang on, I just realized, you're definitely not intelligent, nor thoughtful and perhaps not even fashionable, so I really couldn't care less about your opinion."

Shelby burst into laughter, even one of MG's cronies had a little chuckle.

I led Shelby away as MG growled at her friends for laughing.

Friday

Today during the lunch break, MG was picking on Caroline. Caroline is only new to my school and tends to keep to herself. At first we didn't realize what was happening, but as soon as we did, Shelby and I sat on either side of her.

"Bye Bethany," says Shelby in her best "I'm not scared of you" tone of voice. Ever since our last run in with Bethany, she has avoided us – which we love! Bethany shrugs her shoulders, pokes her tongue out and stomps off in a huff.

That's when we see the tears in Caroline's eyes. She reveals to us that MG has been bullying her almost every day since she arrived at our school. MG has been quietly calling her names in class. So quiet that the teacher and other kids can't hear. And she has been pushing her books off the table as she walks past Caroline's desk.

We tell Caroline that she should tell the teacher what is happening, but apparently MG told Caroline that the teachers at our school hate kids who tell on other kids and that the teachers will only tell her to "just deal with it".

Shelby and I are horrified, I explain to Caroline that bullies often make up stories like this to stop their victims from getting help. "Our teachers are great! If you tell them about Bethany, they'll do their best to stop her," I explained.

Monday

In the morning, Caroline told us that she had taken our advice and spoken to her favorite teacher, Miss Jenkins. At about 9:30 the principal came into the classroom and took Caroline away for about an hour.

Then when he returned with Caroline, he took MG away with him. She walked back into the classroom about 40 minutes later. MG's shoulders were slumped as she quietly returned to her seat. It looked like she had been crying.

At first break, MG kept well away from Caroline. She sat and ate her apple and didn't strut around looking for victims, like she does every other break.

Caroline told us that the principal (I call him Mr. Sausage Nose – he has a really long nose) wanted to know everything that MG had done. She said he was great and he assured her that he would speak to Bethany and that Caroline should come directly to him if she bothered her anymore. Caroline was so happy and couldn't stop thanking us for giving her the courage to speak up. Hi-5's all around.

Bullies 0 – Almost Cool Girls 1!

Tuesday

Mathematics today was so boring! Mr. Wettan or as I like to call him, Mr. Facebook…was at his worst. Unfortunately I have him for both Math and Science, so he is double trouble and doubly bad!

Mr. Facebook (can you guess why?) is only a young teacher. He always has his phone on his desk with Facebook open.

Today he started out with a lesson on fractions and this lesson was starting to look interesting, when his phone made a quiet ding sound. You know the type of noise that lets you know when someone has posted something on your wall. Mid-sentence, Mr. Facebook stops talking and rushes over to his phone. He has a quiet chuckle to himself and suddenly realizes the whole class is sitting there watching him.

He quickly brings up a Math video on the data projector and instructs us to watch it. Then he sits at his desk and taps out messages on his phone for the rest of the lesson.

The video was really boring! The best part was when the principal walked in. Mr. Facebook jumped out of his chair like a startled rabbit! That phone disappeared so fast into his pocket that he may have set a new "hide the phone, speed record".

I think the principal may have seen it. They had a short conversation and although I couldn't make out the words, the tone of voice from the principal didn't sound very happy. When the principal left, the phone stayed in Mr. Facebook's pocket. It was funny because every couple of minutes we could see it vibrating.

Wednesday

The day I've been dreading has finally arrived. I did my best to avoid it! I tried to hide those notes in the bottom of my school bag. I deleted those online school newsletters as soon as I could from our home computer. I even tried to fake being too sick to go to school today, but all that got me was a big spoon of apple cider vinegar, yuck!!!!! Seriously…do normal kids with normal parents have to gulp down that foul tasting vinegar? Uugghh! I'm sure that one day it will turn me into a full-blown zombie!

Sadly, all my best efforts have failed and today Mom is coming to school with me. She is volunteering in the school canteen for a day. Now I love my Mom…it's just when it comes to food she is VERY alternative. We eat enough salads to feed the vast grazing herds of Africa! Mom's idea of junk food is dipping your carrot stick into yoghurt. If it wasn't for Dad, I wouldn't even know about sugar or chocolate.

Our school canteen sells what they call a balanced menu. That means some healthy foods (by normal standards) and some less healthy foods – the really yummy stuff. So I'm a bit worried about how Mom will cope having to serve up food that goes against her healthy food values.

Once at school, Mom puts on her school canteen apron and bids me goodbye, with a cheery, "Be the best you can be, Madonna." That's my Mom, Mrs. Absolutely Positive.

I should have realized something was wrong when I kept getting odd looks as some of my classmates arrived in our room, after putting in their canteen orders.

Lunchtime revealed the full extent of my problem when a group of about ten students approached me as I sat next to Shelby and we began eating our lunch. Tiny (my nickname for David Burrows – the class football hero – who was actually a giant!) stood in front of me. "Maddi, is that your mother in the canteen? The one who is ruining all our lunches!"

"Well," I mumbled, "my mom is in the canteen, she is quite a good cook, I don't think she would RUIN anyone's lunch."

Then the whole group started yelling out their complaints in a storm of jumbled words.

"She made me have brown bread!"

"My ham and salad roll had NO ham!"

"My hotdog had tofu instead of a sausage!"

"I ordered a bag of chips and I got carrot and celery sticks!"

"She scraped all the icing off my cake and said there was enough sugar in the cake!"

"And I wanted a chocolate milkshake and she gave me a green smoothie, gross!!!! It looked like snot!"

This required some quick thinking! I smiled, "Well the good news is that you are all looking a lot healthier and Mom is only working in the canteen once a week for the rest of the term."

All the junk and fatty food fans started groaning and Shelby and I quickly made out escape towards the playground.

I didn't even bother discussing the canteen complaints with mom that night. I know what her response would be and I don't feel like a food lecture. Besides, I have to eat healthy food every day...it won't hurt them to have it once a week!

Saturday

What a day! Mom had invited her friend Demi over for lunch. Demi is an artist and while Mom is a bit of a hippy, Demi is an extreme "free spirit" type of person. Her daughter's name is Star and she is a year older than me. Star doesn't go to school, she is home-schooled. Don't get me wrong, I have nothing against home schooling, in fact I actually think home schooling would be great, but I think Star's education would be very different to my school. Math would probably involve a visit to the local hippy store and adding up the prices of all the weirdo hats. History would probably be watching an old movie. And Science would be gazing at the stars when night falls. Actually, it sounds pretty good!

Anyway I discovered Demi and mom talking in the kitchen as they prepared lunch. Demi greeted me with a cheery, "Hi Maddi, wow, your aura is looking so bright and happy." Then without touching me, she ran her hands around my body, "Your energy levels are magnificent, but I will have to talk to your mom about getting some crystal jewelry to protect you from bad energy."

Mom could see that I'm feeling a bit uncomfortable with all this attention. She breaks in, "Maddi, Star is in your room, you should go and say hi."

My mind races! Star is in my room. Who said she could go in there? My room is full of my private stuff. I race down to save my privacy.

TOO LATE!!!!!

Star is laying on my bed reading my diary! She looks over the top of the book as I burst into my room. Before she even says, "Hi Maddi," I rip my diary from her hands. She tries to snatch it back, "Come on Maddi, it was just getting interesting!"

Star is an imposing sight, tall for her age with her dyed jet black hair long on one side and almost shaved on the other side. She has multiple earrings and a fake tattoo on her arm (at least I think it is fake) and a stud in both of her eyebrows. I clutch my diary to my chest and screech, "How dare you read my diary, it's private!"

"Not anymore," she responds with a smirk. "Don't worry Maddi, I'm not interested in your dull little school dramas, my life is much more interesting," snarled Star.

At that moment Mom arrived, "Come on girls, we are going for lunch." Good timing Mom, Star and I were about to have our own version of wrestle mania.

On the trip to lunch, Mom and Demi chatted constantly, while Star and I sat in the back seat – in total silence!

In the restaurant, things continued much the same, until in a moment of unexpected meanness, Star tips her glass of juice into my lap. I squeal as the cold liquid hits my thighs. Finally Mom and Demi stop talking. They both grab some napkins and start to try and soak up the mess. The waiter comes over too and helps clean up the juice. He even replaces Star's drink.

Star keeps saying that she is sorry. I know she doesn't mean it. Mom says, "Don't worry dear, accidents happen." Star gives me her best fake smile and winks at me. I feel like tipping my juice over Star's head but show some restraint and decide to wait for a better chance for revenge.

The meals arrive, Star and I both have nachos with little side dishes of sour cream and chilli sauce. The chilli sauce is in a bottle that looks like a soda bottle. Star announces that she needs to go to the bathroom and I see my chance. As the waiter goes past I ask if I can I swap my chilli sauce for extra hot chilli sauce. I think he feels sorry for me and rushes off to change the sauce bottles. I quickly swap it with the bottle next to Star's plate.

Star returns and grabs the extra hot sauce bottle and dumps the whole lot over her nachos. She must be hungry, as she quickly scoffs two large mouthfuls of food into her mouth. Suddenly her eyes widen and she starts to cough. I guess that the extra hot chilli sauce is starting to take effect. While she is distracted I hand her the second bottle of chilli sauce, she thinks it is her soft drink and takes a large gulp. Her eyes bulge like some type of wild cartoon character and she explodes. A mouthful of sauce and nachos flies across the table. A bit hits Mom, but most of it splashes onto Demi. Needless to say, after that, lunch is over.

The ride home is pretty quiet, except for me munching my nachos and Star's occasional coughing and whimpering that her mouth is on fire. The waiter put my nachos in a take-away container and with a wink said, "Careful with that sauce."

Demi and Star head off in their car as soon as we got home. Mom gave me a stern look and asked if I had anything to do with what happened at lunch. I just smiled and replied, "I think those nachos had a dash of karma." Mom screwed up her face, trying to work out what I had meant. Then she shrugged her shoulders, gave me a kiss and went downstairs.

Monday

D is for disaster!
D is also for devastated!

Today after school the worst thing ever happened. Mom called me into the kitchen, Dad was already sitting at the breakfast table. Dad's normal happy smiling face had disappeared, replaced by a very sad mask. A glance at Mom revealed that her expression closely matched Dad's.

A million things raced through my mind!
Had they discovered I changed a C in Math on my last report card into a B with skillful use of a fine black marker?

Could it be that zombies are real and we are the last humans left?

Or, was I adopted and today I was to be returned to my rightful parents...the King and Queen of some European country?

Wrong!!!!!
Much worse!!!!!!

Mom and Dad haven't been getting along very well for the last few months and they have decided to separate for a while. There were tears all round, but Mom and Dad assured me they both still love me and we would still be a family, although Dad would be going away for a while.

I felt sad when Dad left that night, as did Mom. We cried on each other's shoulders. Dad had promised to contact us each day and Mom said she believed Dad would be back. She said it was the stress of his job causing him to be sad. True to his word, Dad calls or emails us every day and I just hope we'll all be back together one day.

I don't want to say…D is for divorce!

2 Weeks Later…
Tuesday

I haven't written in my diary for a while. I've been missing Dad and so has Mom, so I've spent more time keeping her company. For a while Mrs. Absolutely Positive lost her shine and sparkle, but we have both settled down now. Dad still contacts us every day and even though he isn't here, he is still part of my life.

The funniest thing happened at school today in Math. My History teacher's nickname is Mr. Oscar…because he is always super grumpy! He reminds me of Oscar the grouch from Sesame Street. He even has those big googly eyes behind his glasses, just like the Oscar puppet.

Anyway, in his normal grouchy way he made everyone shift their seats so we weren't sitting with our friends. I ended up sitting between Bethany Barker (MG – short for mean girl) and a boy called Justin Smithers. I haven't had a lot to do with Justin, but have heard some of the "less kind" boys call him "Dustbin" rather than Justin.

That unfortunate name goes back to last year in my English class. Our teacher was a very young and pretty lady who was always beautifully dressed with perfect make-up and hair. So obviously I called her Miss Barbie!

Miss Barbie was quite a good teacher but was rather obsessed with neatness and cleanliness. Sometimes she would stop in the middle of a lesson to straighten the pencils and books on a kid's desk. She even had a bottle of hand sanitizer on her desk that she used every time after she touched our work books.

After lunch and playtimes she would spray an air freshener around the room. And she would always say the same thing, "We really don't want to be smelling all those sweaty bodies and foot odors all afternoon, do we children?"

Sometimes on particularly hot days she would tip some of her perfume onto a tissue and hold it up to her nose to protect her delicate senses from her foul-smelling students. So you get the picture...Miss Barbie is one delicate princess!

In her classroom the desks are always perfectly arranged in groups of six. One day as Miss Barbie moved around the room, I saw her nose begin to twitch and then her perfect face transformed into a grimace. With a puzzled look she slowly moved around the room, stopping at each desk and sniffing gently. "Does someone need to go to the bathroom?" she asks in her delicate sweet voice. She obviously thinks one of us has let off a smelly fart. Naturally nobody responded. Everyone put their heads down and focused on their work. Miss Barbie continued to sniff around the room.

"There is a really bad smell in here somewhere," she announced loudly with her sweet voice turning shrill as her delicate senses are assaulted by the smell. This time a few kids responded that they can smell something bad too. Miss Barbie starts a more intensive sniffing campaign, moving from one group to another.

Finally she returned to the group next to mine. In that group are 3 girls and 3 boys, one of the boys is Justin Smithers. She calls each of the kids out to the front of the class, one at a time, for a whispered conversation. I manage to just hear the words, "Are you sure you don't need to use the bathroom," as she talks to each of the kids. Miss Barbie does another circuit of the room before returning to the same group.

This time she starts going around the group instructing each student to open their desk. Miss Barbie has a quick look and a big sniff and then moves onto the next desk. She's found nothing so far and there are only two kids left, Justin and another boy.

Following Miss Barbie's instructions, Justin opens his desk wide and Miss Barbie takes a big sniff. She recoils in horror and takes two steps back. Her perfect face is pinched up into a scowl. She holds her nose as she uses a ruler to poke around in Justin's desk. With the tips of her fingers she lifts a plastic wrapped item from the desk, it oozes and drips and a disgusting stench floods the room.

Miss Barbie runs from the room, still clutching the stinking mess in her hand and making retching noises as she leaves. Five minutes later, Mr. Sausage Nose – the principal, walks in and announces he will be taking the class as Miss Barbie has gone home sick.

After class the kids are giving Justin a bit of a hard time for causing the stink. He explains that he hadn't finished his hot dog at lunchtime so he had hidden it in his desk, intending to eat it in class while the teacher wasn't looking.

It could not have stunk that bad…just from lunchtime. We saw that it was starting to decompose, turning to mush!

Justin's mouth opened wide, he went white, "Oh no, it wasn't my hot dog from today, it was a hamburger from about 3 months ago! I forgot about it."

Apparently Justin couldn't smell it because he had his nose broken twice playing football and the injury had totally destroyed his sense of smell. And that is unfortunately how Justin got to be called Dustbin by some of our nastier class members.

Anyway, here I sit between Justin and Mean Girl, as Mr. Oscar fires lightning fast questions around the room. I follow the standard "avoid being picked to answer questions" tactics, appearing to listen intently and making no eye contact with the teacher and nodding wisely when someone else answered correctly.

When suddenly Mean Girl jabs me in the ribs with her sharp and boney elbow. I give an involuntary "oomph" as I double over in pain and surprise. That's when I make my mistake, I panic and look up to see if Mr. Oscar has heard me. Bad mistake! Our eyes lock! EYE CONTACT! Oh no….

"Right Maddi, next question is yours," snaps Mr. Oscar. Panic overtakes me, my pulse is beating faster than a speeding bullet. Here comes the question, I hold my breath, trying to focus. "What is the bluzen dinky xyt24 62536477flmkjqu," he asks. At least that is what it sounded like to me.

My… "I don't know" response gets a swift reaction. "I'll see you at lunchtime for some extra work, Maddi."

I steal a glance at Mean Girl and she gives me a self-satisfied smirk while poking her tongue at me.

Justin asks for a loan of a blue coloring pencil and I hand it over with a smile. As I work on my assignment, I notice that Justin is using my pencil for NON-coloring purposes. First he uses the non-sharpened end to give both his ears a good clean out, then he does a bit of exploration of his right nostril. It's hard to be sure but I think I see a little green thing on the end of my pencil.

Justin returns my pencil with a "thanks".

I reply, "Pop it on my desk." After a while I 'accidently'

knock the pencil off my desk onto the floor. I don't want to hurt Justin's feelings, but there is NO WAY that I am going to put my fingers on that germ-covered pencil ever again! The cleaners can have that one, they wear gloves when they pick up stuff from the classroom floor, so I know they won't catch anything.

Mean Girl must have seen me drop the pencil off my desk because she suddenly swoops down and picks it up. Why at this precise moment in world history does Mean Girl decide to be nice to me? I'm wracking my brain to think of reasons why I don't want the pencil back…without revealing the truth. If she knew why I didn't want the pencil back, she might use that information to tease Justin.

No need to worry! Mean Girl waggles the pencil at me and sneers, "Was this yours? Well not anymore, this is my favorite color."

As well as being a bully and a generally unlikeable person…Mean Girl has another off-putting habit. She chews on things – her fingers, her ruler, the ends of her hair and today she has something else to chew on…the end of my pencil.

GROSS! She has a good chew and I can't help but snigger. She hears me and turns and sticks even more of my pencil into her mouth to chew on. I laugh even more. A confused look shows on Mean Girl's face, me laughing was not the reaction she expected.

I decide not to tell her why I am laughing, not today…maybe another time when she is being a bully. It's so funny that I even manage to get through my lunchtime detention with a smile on my face.

Thursday

Science is looking interesting today. Mr. Facebook is taking our lesson in the actual science lab! There are beakers and test tubes and Bunsen burners and bottles of chemicals labeled with A, B, C and D on each of the tables.

Naturally Shelby and I grab a table together. Our table is at the far back corner of the room near a window. Unfortunately, it is a bit hard to hear Mr. Facebook from our table as he is demonstrating what to do from the front of the room.

Mr. Facebook is on fire (well not really on fire) and teaching a great lesson. He has us mixing chemicals and stuff and creating all kinds of exciting reactions like clouds of colored steam and popping bubbles bursting out of beakers.

The whole class is really involved and having fun. To be honest, we are all being a bit too noisy because the activities are so exciting.

Mr. Facebook announces that our last activity can be a little dangerous and to listen and watch carefully. He starts giving instructions on how to measure out quantities of different chemicals.

In our far corner, Shelby and I are struggling to hear his instructions. When he measured chemical C...we couldn't tell if he said 15mls or 50mls. So I went to the front to ask him. Just as I got there, he pulled out his phone, obviously he had heard a Facebook notification. "Excuse me," I asked politely, "did you say 15 or 50?" His attention is firmly fixed on his phone now and he answers, "Yes" to my question. Even I know that "yes" isn't the right answer. I repeat the question.

Mr. Facebook is now typing away on his phone and if possible…giving me even less attention. "50!" he snarls, followed by, "get back to your table and do your experiment."

I go back to the table and tell Shelby he said 50. She looks doubtful but what can we do? We start to combine our chemicals into the one large beaker. First chemical A and then chemical B. We hesitate as nothing has happened. The group at the next table have just finished pouring in chemical C. From their beaker we see a puff of smoke and hear a loud pop.

That doesn't look too scary, so I grab the 50ml of chemical C that we have already measured out and pour it into the beaker (containing the other chemicals). I'm holding the beaker in my left hand, watching it closely. I can see the mixture of chemicals bubbling up, heading towards the top of the beaker. If the group next to us had a puff of smoke…we have our own little nuclear bomb mushroom cloud happening. The bubbly chemicals are about to spill over the side of the beaker! No way am I going to let that toxic brew touch my fingers! The only place I can see to dump it is in the waste paper basket next to our table.

I toss the beaker like an extreme basketball shot. The beaker lands in the basket and seconds later there is an extremely loud bang, followed by even more smoke pouring from the bin. The smoke is quickly drifting across the classroom. The loud bang has finally managed to draw the attention of Mr. Facebook from his phone. He gazes in stunned horror at the room rapidly filling with smoke. Finally he screams, "Get out, FIRE!" Everyone panics and runs for the door. Mr. Facebook hits the fire alarm on his way out of the building.

The Principal looks crazed, ordering everyone to evacuate all the school buildings. Soon our class is joined on the athletics field by the whole school. I sit listening to the sound of approaching fire trucks.

Once the all-clear signal is given, Mr. Facebook marches me up to Mr. Sausage Nose's office and firmly lays the blame on me. I sit in the chair outside his office, waiting for my mom.

When Mom arrives I try to explain what happened. But Mr. Sausage Nose keeps interrupting me, saying how no other group had any problems. Mr. Facebook had told him that I wasn't listening and that is the reason why I added way too much of the chemical. When I tried to tell Mr. Sausage Nose how the teacher was on the phone instead of answering my question, he went on to praise Mr. Facebook for having the sense to use his personal phone to ring the fire and rescue. He said that if it hadn't been for his quick thinking and action…I could have burned down the whole school. "That's why he had his phone out Maddi, you must be confused," he said sternly.

"Mom, this is so unfair, it's really not my fault. I'm telling you the truth!" I shouted.

The principal started to tell Mom that I would be suspended for 4 weeks for my actions.

To my shock, my mom butted in, raising her voice, "My daughter does NOT lie! She will not be suspended, we are moving to a new school." She grabbed me by the hand and stormed out of the office.

As we drove away, Mrs. Absolutely Positive simply said,

"Maddi, don't worry, there are plenty of lovely schools to go to. There is a silver lining to every cloud of smoke."

And that's why I'm heading to my next adventure in 'My New School'.

Maddi

Find out what happens next in
in Book 2 of

Diary of Mr. Tall, Dark and Handsome Book 1 -
My Life Has Changed

Sunday

Hey diary…wow this feels really weird. It's kind of like I'm talking to myself. But I really need someone to talk to, so here we go.

The worse thing ever happened last week.

Can't do this.

***

Wednesday

Let's try again. Last week my Mom died. She gave me one of her big kisses, combed my hair and said, "Have a great day, love you." Then she got into her car and drove off.

That was the last time I ever saw her. It's NOT FAIR!!!!!!!!!!!! Why did she have to go? I WANT her BACK! I NEED her BACK NOW!

I feel really sad.

Friday

Everything is dull. I miss her smile. She was the funniest person ever. She could make anyone laugh. Dad is really sad too. He pretends he is okay, but I hear him crying at night. The days dissolve into each other. I feel so alone. Sometimes my heart actually hurts and my throat feels sore and closes over. It's kind of like I'm in a horror movie and all the humans have turned to ants, so busy running around, making noises, going through the motions of life.

It has been two weeks now.

My Mother

Monday

I wasn't looking forward to school today. You see, I'm not that special. Actually I am pretty average. I'm not a jock, in fact I don't really like football at all. Football is really big at my school. The boys on the footy team are like heroes and don't they know it.

I only have a couple of really close friends at school, James and Jeremy. We hang out at lunchtime and talk about movies and the latest games. We all play on Xbox Live and our favorite game is Halo.

Mom was really proud of me. She told me that I'm smart and kind. Dad is really into sport - footy, basketball and baseball are his passions. I don't really relate all that well to Dad. We have different interests and sometimes I think he is disappointed to have me as his son.

I also like computer graphics. Last year I got an A!!!! Mom was so proud; she made me a computer shaped cake to celebrate.

Oh, something funny happened today. We got a new girl in our class. Her name is Madonna and she seems really nice. You should have seen her entry into the classroom. It was classic! Our teacher kept going on and on about how much fun our classroom is and then she sat her next to Burt. Now I don't want to sound mean, but Burt is a little different. Last year he tried to set a record for the biggest number of boogers he could stick onto the bottom of his desk. And his breath always smells of tuna. Gross!!!!

This poor new girl sat down next to Burt and slumped her shoulders. Then she peeked around the room and that was when our eyes met. I smiled. And she smiled back.

Tuesday

Swimming Day. Oh joy! Remember how I told you I wasn't that good at sports, well that includes swimming. I'm in the average group; yes we try to swim up and down, up and down, while our swim coach flirts with the lifeguard. All the girls think he is handsome, he's tall, blonde, tanned and it is obvious he works out at the gym…a lot!

Once I asked my swim coach how I could improve my stroke and she told me not to worry about it because, "You'll never be any good anyway." So I just put my head down and do my best. Up, down, up, down….

Even though I am quite tall, I haven't gone through puberty yet. Yep, you know what that means - no hair. There is a really mean boy in our class called Damian and he is really hairy!!!! He even has some growing on his chin. The worst part about the whole swimming thing is the change room. I don't like stripping off in front of other people, so I always try to sneak into the toilet to change. We aren't allowed to do that. The teachers reckon that we are hogging the toilets and someone might actually need to go. There are only two cubicles and today they were both taken. So I stripped off as quickly as I could and kept the towel around my waist.

Damian grabbed my towel and horsewhipped my butt with it. He yelled, "Well check out our little boy, when are you going to grow some hair and be a man like me!"

I cracked. I pushed him and he fell back, just as Mr Albert walked into the change rooms. So now I have to do a detention with him tomorrow after school. Great!

One of the girls dropped their undies on the way into the pool. They had Dora the Explorer on them. Of course NOBODY owned up. When are teachers going to learn that holding up a pair of undies and asking who owns them NEVER works!!!!

A few moments later, the loud speaker blasted across the pool area that Madonna's undies were at the canteen. That poor girl! All the cool girls laughed, they can be so mean and cruel. Then the jocks joined in, they can be so dumb and horrible. A few of the nerdy kids were wondering what all the fuss was about and the rest of us just felt sorry for her.

Wednesday

Some days are worse than others. Today was a really bad day. I feel sad. I miss my Mom.

This morning I decided to clean the house. Seriously, I think we need to buy a whole heap of plastic plates, cups and cutlery. Then we can eat and throw away the mess.

I went into Mom's room to dust. I can still smell her. Dad hasn't put away her clothes and belongings yet. Everything is still laid out on her dressing table. Today I looked through her drawer. She had kept everything I have ever made for her. You know all those drawings and cards for Mothers' Day, Christmas and her birthdays. She even has a little case with all my baby teeth and a pasta bracelet I made for her at Kindy.

I also found a silk purse with a message on it. It said, 'For Richard'. My heart pounded as I carefully opened the purse. Inside was a beautiful and very old fob watch and a note.

I read the note:

My Dearest Richard

If you are reading this note, then I have passed on. Don't be sad my beautiful boy. I will always be with you in your heart. You are special in so many ways, be strong and enjoy your life.

This watch was given to me by my mother. It has been handed down through the generations and is over 100 years old. Please take care of it. It is very special and my Mom told me it has special powers. I haven't worked out what those powers are yet and it may just be a myth. Your Dad didn't want me investigating it, he said it was all a bunch of baloney, but I'm not so sure.

Do you remember Grandma Mary? When I was young, she would sit around the fire with me and tell the most amazing stories. My favorite was a story about her visiting ancient Egypt and working in the Pharaoh's harem. She served the Queen and saved her life when the Romans invaded the palace. She really was an amazing woman and an incredible storyteller.

Just before she died, she told me that one day I would be in charge of the family heirloom, a fob watch that I could use to travel the world and find my own stories.

My plan is to do this when you finish school. But if something should happen to me, then this precious watch will become yours.

Please don't ignore it like I have so far. Explore it. It may all be a story…but we won't know until one of us tries it.

Grandma Mary told me to rub it with my fingers, while closing my eyes and focusing on where and when I want to go. She told me not to be scared.

I love you Richard.

Mom xx

I read the note four times. It didn't really make sense…what did the watch do? But just knowing it was part of my Mom and her wacky family made it the most valuable possession I have ever laid my eyes on.

I took it into my room and put it under my pillow.

Wednesday

Last night was one long dream. My Mom and Grandma Mary visited me. They told me that I was the chosen one. In my dream I had the fob watch around my neck. It was warm to touch and sparkling.

I travelled to Ancient Egypt in the blink of an eye, with Grandma Mary and she introduced me to the Queen of Egypt. I worked as a guard for the Queen and her two children. We travelled in a camel caravan to inspect her husband's latest pyramid. I rode beside her on a chariot with a spear in my hand. When we got there, the guards lifted her onto a litter and carried her to inspect the workers.

I actually thought she was pretty lazy! This is a picture I drew that shows the Queen being carried.

There were hundreds of workers, carving rocks and boulders into bricks and loading them onto carts to transport to the pyramid. It was boiling hot, the sun beat down on me and sweat ran down my back. I felt really sorry for the workers; they were dressed in rags and had no protection from the glaring sun.

Then a horn sounded. Everyone stopped and pointed to the horizon. There was a low brown cloud. But it wasn't a rain cloud, it was dust and it kept rising higher and higher. The workers started to run away and the Queen and her children were quickly put onto horses so they could be rushed to safety. The guards and some of the workers formed a line and waited. I had no idea what was happening.

Then I started to hear a thud-thud noise. Out of the dust came hundreds of men on horses and chariots racing towards us. The men had round shields, long sharp sticks and armor on their bodies. They were screaming words that I could not understand.

This is what the chariots looked liked:

by: Richard Jones

My mouth went dry, my heart pounded in my chest and my mind almost went blank. Grandma Mary grabbed my arm and told me to wake; this was not my fight or story. "Wake-up Richard!"

I opened my eyes and I was in my bedroom safe and sound, with the fob watch around my neck. Strangely it was warm and seemed to be very bright.

What a dream! Talk about an over-active imagination! But it had seemed so real, like I was really there. I rolled over, said goodnight to Mom and went to sleep.

School was okay today. Jeremy's cousin, Gretel is in our class. She seems like a really nice girl; pretty quiet, but kind and thoughtful. Her family sent Dad and I a sympathy card. Today I talked to her for the first time and thanked her. She was so funny, her face went really red and she stammered that she was really sorry for my loss. I think I'd like to be her friend. She is the only girl in the class who is making an effort to make the new girl, Madonna, feel welcome.

Seriously, some of the kids in our class are so mean. I'm not sure if they are even aware…but they really know how to put people down. They act really tough, like they don't care. I think that secretly they just want to fit in and maybe they are scared to stand up to the tough kids. What is that saying? *If you can't beat them…join them.* If you have to be mean spirited and nasty to get attention, then it isn't worth it. Funny thing is, when you get them by themselves, most of them are quite nice. Peer pressure, man does it cause problems! And if I have to act like the footy jocks to be in the cool group, they can have it.

Thursday

Good night diary. Nothing to report today. Oh, except that Madonna smiled at me. Sweet dreams!

Oh, and tonight I'm putting the fob watch in my drawer, just in case I dream again.

Night Mom, I love you.

***

Friday

Our first cooking session with Miss Moffat. I am in a group with Gretel and Madonna (the new girl). Gretel is pretty confident and seems to know what she is doing. Just as we have finished cutting up the vegetables and chicken, a phone call comes through, asking for Gretel to go to the office so she can go home.

Panic started to overtake me. But then Madonna stepped up. She seemed so confident. We were the first to finish and our dish looked delicious. That was until Miss Moffat tasted it. The chicken was raw! It wasn't cooked through.

Miss Moffat's face turned white, then green. She burped and then projectile vomited. It landed on my shirt. It was like being in a horror movie. When I realized what was happening, I jumped back, but it was too late. I was covered in vomit.

I didn't know what to say, so I just walked out of the classroom and went to the toilets. The smell attacked my nostrils and when I took off my shirt I found a hunk of raw chicken. I felt hot and clammy and then I started to throw up as well. At least my vomit went into the toilet!

Sunday

Lately my head has been really itchy. Dad told me that sometimes stress and nerves can make your scalp itchy. So naturally I believed him and didn't give it a second thought. I went to the hairdressers today. How embarrassing! I've got head lice! The hairdresser, who is really young and pretty, started to comb my hair and then she stopped. She called over an older lady and they both started looking closely at my scalp. The older lady announced in a loud voice, "You've got lice! We can't cut your hair; you'll have to treat your head lice first."

The young hairdresser looked at me, smiled and shrugged her shoulders, as the older one kept going on about different treatments I could buy from the chemist. Everyone in the salon looked at me, like I was a leper. I could feel my face catching on fire. I looked in the mirror and my face had gone a tomato shade of red. I left as quickly as I could.

Then I had to go to the chemist and buy some treatment. I chose one and tried to hide it as I went to the counter. A few people were being served, so I waited until they had left and quickly gave it to the girl at the checkout.

She tried to scan it and it didn't register, so she pulled over a microphone and asked for a price check on the Nitfree Head lice Treatment. I felt like melting into the cracks between the tiles. Then she asked if I wanted a bag. Hello, of course I wanted a bag!

I had to do it myself when I got home. Mom used to do so much for me, she was so loving. I combed the lotion through my hair. With the number of lice I found, I could have started up my own lice circus. Imagine that, The Amazing Nit Show brought to you by Richard Jones!

Now where did I pick them up from? Maybe Burt, he is always scratching. I make a mental note, never sit close to him or let him use my hat, EVER!!!!

Monday

The funniest thing happened at school today. Well it was funny and really embarrassing. In English my teacher collected our homework on the Merchant of Venice. I really don't like reading old stories. He started reading the new girl's reflections. It said something like this:

The quality of mercy is not strained, but falls like the gentle rain. I wish Mr. Albert would give me some mercy and seat me next to hunky Richard Jones.

I felt my face blush. I'm sure I looked like Elmo! Everyone started laughing and cheering. I felt like I was on fire. My hands broke into an instant sweat. I looked at Madonna and her face was also bright red. She looked in shock!

Our teacher asked who is Mr. Albert. Madonna just stumbled over that question, saying it was just her imagination. Thank goodness the bell went and we could both escape outside. I didn't see her during the lunch break, she disappeared very quickly.

Of course everyone was talking about it during lunch. I was constantly teased about being hunky. We guessed that she called our teacher Mr. Albert because he has frizzy hair like Albert Einstein. She really does have a great sense of humor. Just thinking about her brings a smile to my face.

This is all kind of weird for me. No girl has ever shown me the least bit of interest. I'm not cool and I'm certainly not hunky. But knowing that she might think that, does make me feel pretty special.

After lunch we went to our art class. Madonna sat on the opposite side of the room to me and kept her head down. I wanted to talk to her and tell her that everything was okay, but she wouldn't make eye contact. I feel so sorry for her.

Nathan came over to me and slapped me on the back saying, "Hey hunky, how's it going?" I just ignored him, he isn't very nice. Little did I know that he was actually playing a trick on me. He had put a sign on my back and it said:

Madonna Loves Richard the Hunk!

Unfortunately my friends walked out before me and didn't see it. I walked all the way down the hall and to the bus stop before I realized that something was wrong. It was the constant sniggering and wolf whistling which followed me that told me something was wrong. Why do kids have to be so cruel? Luckily Madonna didn't see it, she was one of the first to leave the classroom. She took off like a rocket!

I don't like being teased, but I have to admit, I'm kind of thrilled that she might like me.

Saturday

Dad sat in front of the TV all day...watching sport. I spent most of the day in my room, going through old photo albums. My Mom was such a beautiful woman. She had the best smile!

I'm really good on the computer and I love to make graphics. So today I scanned pictures of my Mom and made a video collage, it looks awesome. My favorite one is when she first held me in hospital. She looked so young and soft. Her eyes were so beautiful, full of love. I also found some funny ones. Mom was such a clown...always pulling faces and photo bombing. I showed it to Dad, but he started to tear up and walked away.

Then I went for a bike ride.

Sunday

When I woke up this morning, Dad had already gone. He left a note saying that he had work to finish at his office and would be home for lunch.

Hmmmm…….

What to do?

I decided to go for a bike ride. I love going down this really big hill near my school. The wind flies through my hair and I go really fast. I just have to watch out for cars backing out of their driveways.

At the bottom of the hill I skidded to a stop, got off my bike and took my drink out of my backpack.

"What are you up to?" said a familiar voice from behind. It was Ted Martin, a family friend who is in my class. Now I wouldn't call Ted a close friend, but we have a mutual respect thing going. You see Ted lost his Mom when he was really young. He can barely remember her. My Mom used to bake for their family every weekend and she always invited Ted to my birthday parties and for plays after school. After Mom passed (I find it really hard to use the word died) he would come round after school and just sit with me, watching TV. We didn't talk about it, but one day he looked at me and said, "I know." Those two words said it all.

The other kids at school don't really like Ted. He can be really mean, but I think it is because he is looking for attention. His Dad works really long hours at the local brick works and he isn't very loving or kind. Mom used to say that Ted was trying to make himself feel better by putting others down. She tried to talk to him about it, but I don't think he understood.

He does stupid things like pouring glue into tidy boxes, sticking gum under other people's desks, throwing rubbers during class and breaking other kids' rulers. Lately he has started taking food from some of the kids. He is almost becoming a "stand over man". The worst thing is that he does it so meanly and only takes the good stuff, like cakes and biscuits. Last Friday when he went off looking for robbery victims during lunch time, I casually strolled over and looked in his lunch box. There was nothing in there. Maybe he is stealing because he is hungry. I feel really sorry for him.

Ted and I went for a walk in the bush near a creek at the bottom of the school. We were looking for little fish in the creek when we saw movement in the bush. We bobbed down and watched carefully. You wouldn't believe who it was, our Deputy Principal and her husband. She was going off at him because he had forgotten the bait for their fishing expedition. He kept saying, "Yes dear" – "No dear" – "I know dear." It was so funny! Ted and I looked at each other and our bodies started to shake from trying to stop the laughter escaping from our mouths. Anyway they kept on walking along the path. Funny how some people are like that, bossy at work and bossy on the weekends! That poor man! If I was him I would wear ear plugs.

We played around for a bit longer, seeing who could skip the flat rocks as we tossed them across the water. My best rock skipped 6 times, pretty impressive! I had to leave because Dad would be home soon, but Ted was going to hang around for a bit longer, his Dad was playing golf with his friends (he does that every Sunday).

Monday

Guess what, there is a school competition and you can win passes to Water World Park. I really want to win! It would be so much fun. I love waterslides!!!!

***

Tuesday

I entered the waterslide competition today. I'm in a group with Gretel and Madonna (she told me to call her Maddi for short). The girls are really keen to win too. I hope I don't let them down. They asked me to take care of the graphics. I'm kind of excited about this because I'm pretty good at designing on the computer. I also like painting and drawing pictures, so that will definitely help as well.

I really like Maddi. She is really pretty, she has great hair and really beautiful eyes; when she smiles her face lights up. And she gives off a really positive vibe. When I am near her I feel funny inside, a little nervous and a little excited. I can't wait to go to school tomorrow and tell her about my ideas for our project.

Wednesday

Maddi and Gretel really like my ideas! Maddi told me that I am very creative and smart. This is SO COOL! That is what my Mom used to say to me. I know that Mom would really like Maddi.

During lunch time I was about to walk around the corner when I heard my name. So I stopped and listened. It was Maddi talking to Gretel. They were saying how happy they are that I'm in their group for the competition. Then I heard Gretel say, "And he's such a nice boy." Awww that's so nice. But then I heard something that almost made me fall over. Maddi told Gretel that she likes to make up names for people and my secret name is Mr. Tall, Dark and Handsome. I didn't know what to do. I know I blushed to the deepest shade of purple possible. Then I held my breath and slowly took a few steps backwards, spun around and quickly walked away.

Surely she is joking. Me…tall, dark and handsome, it has to be a joke! Secretly, I hope it isn't. Maddi makes me feel good. She makes me feel happy. I think I like her a lot.

Thursday

Today was try-out day for school sport. There was a choice of basketball (great for all the giants), football (the jocks have that one stitched up) and soccer. So I decided to try out for soccer, it isn't as rough and I thought I'd have a chance.

I have a tendency to daydream. I glanced over at the girls' groups and saw Maddi holding a soccer ball. I was imagining myself being a school soccer star thinking how Maddi would be so impressed and wasn't really listening to the teacher giving directions. So off I walked with a group of boys. We were divided into two teams and walked out onto the field. That was when I noticed some of the boys around me. Why were the jocks trying out for soccer? Where were the soccer nets? Why wasn't the ball round?

Then the ball came flying into my hands. Oh no! It's a football! That is when Dan (they call him Dan the man) came bearing down on me. He hit me like a ten-ton truck. The ball flew out of my hands and I was flat on my back. I heard the whistle blow and saw faces looking down on me. They picked me up and carried me off the field. Dazed but still alive (only just) I walked to the benches and thought about my mistake. In future, I'm going to listen!

The really bad thing is that by the time I recovered and went over to the soccer try-outs, the teams were filled. So that means I have to do alternate sport. All the kids call it *reject sport*. There are five choices for reject sport: yoga, gym, ball skills, history club, math games and computer graphics. We had to put a number next to each activity from 1 to 6. I put one next to computer graphics and 6 next to all the other choices. Then I drew a smiley face next to my top choice. I hope the teachers understand that I REALLY want to do computer graphics.

Friday

Oh NO! I can't believe it...they put me in the history club group. My friends are in ball skills and computer graphics. How can they justify having stupid things like history club in reject sport? I told Dad, but he just grunted. I'm really NOT looking forward to next Thursday! Seriously!!!!!

**

Saturday

Today I worked on our project for the Water World Competition. The pictures look great! The girls are going to love them. When I grow up I think I'd like to have my own business. I could design logos, banners and pictures for websites. That would be so much fun.

When I was little I wanted to be a rubbish collection man. Every time the rubbish truck came past I'd run to the front yard and watch. Then one day, Mom took me out to meet him. He let me smell inside the truck. Boy did it stink! He told me to choose another job or have that smell in my nose for the rest of my life. At the time, I thought he was a bit mean to destroy my dream of becoming a rubbish man. But over the years, every time Mom and I saw a rubbish truck we would look at each other and laugh.

Who knows...I might end up being the next Steve Jobs. Imagine inventing a new type of computer system! How exciting would that be! Or designing a new game or making animations for a film. See, I told you I am a dreamer. ☺

Sunday

Today I asked Dad about the fob watch. He had a really black look on his face. "Richard, your Mom came from a crazy family. They had lots of weird ideas and used to make up stupid stories. It is just a watch. It has no special powers."

This was what I expected him to say. What do I do now? Should I just put it away and forget about it? I struggled with this thought all day long. Grandma Mary was a bit weird...but Mom wasn't. And in her letter she said that she wanted me to explore it. Dad probably said the same thing to her. So I grabbed the watch and put it in my pocket, climbed an oak tree in the backyard and asked Mom what to do. I squeezed my eyes shut and waited for an answer, but nothing came.

I held the watch in my hand and gently rubbed it. I thought about Richard the Lion Heart during his crusade to win back the holy land. The year was 1191. My history teacher had told us gruesome stories about both sides. I was thinking about the Christians marching to Jerusalem and then...

My vision blurred and I felt like I was falling through a tunnel of darkness. All around me were a mish-mash of sounds, some voices talking in languages I didn't understand, animal noises and a variety of banging, crashing and creaking sounds.

Next thing I knew I had hit the ground with a thump and I laid there stunned. I must've fallen out of the tree. As I lay on the ground in front of my eyes there wasn't the soft green grass of my backyard... but a dry dusty mixture of gravel, sand and larger rocks.

What was going on, where was I? "Move boy!" growled a rough, loud voice. I looked up to see a medieval knight mounted on a huge horse almost walking on top of me. I rolled to the side, out of his way and came to a halt against the block wall. As I scrambled to my feet, I looked up at the wall. It was huge and stretched up above me. It wasn't just a wall, it was the inside wall of an olden day castle. Above me I could see soldiers in chain mail walking along the top and above them on two poles were large flags that flapped in the breeze. One of the flags was red with three yellow lions on it. The other flag was blue with a white cross.

"Which way to the palace?" I just stared dumbly at him, stunned by what was going on. "What's wrong boy, have the Saracens cut out your tongue?" asked the gruff old knight. His fellow knight nudged his horse closer and eyed me up and down. "Those are strange clothes you have on boy, where'd you come from?" he asked. "I'm from Harper Valley sir," I replied. The sir just popped out, but it did seem appropriate when talking to a large man in armor with a sword towering over me on a huge horse.

"Sir Edward," said the second knight, "there is something strange about this fellow, he could be a spy for the Saracens, we should take him with us to the palace." "Walter get a rope on him and bring him with us." Suddenly I noticed a third man dressed in long robes as he came riding towards us on a small horse. He looked younger than the other two. He pulled the rope from his saddle swinging a loop of it in the air and launched it at me. The loop landed around my neck and the men watched as Walter pulled it tight. I reached up to try and pull it off when all three started to ride off. I was pulled in a stumbling run behind them. I forgot about pulling the rope from my neck and just concentrated on staying on my feet, petrified I would be dragged behind the horse if I fell.

For about 10 minutes I stumbled along behind Walter and his horse. To make it even worse at one point the horse decided to go to the toilet. Despite my best dodging efforts I ended up with bits of horse manure in my hair and on my face and down my shirt front and on my shoes. As I was led through the narrow dusty streets I gazed around in wonder. There were ramshackle markets, people in unusual clothing and dead animals hanging up and being sold. It was like being in a scene from a movie.

It must be Grandma Mary's fob watch. Somehow I had traveled back in time. This must be what mom was trying to tell me about. Maybe all those stories that my grandmother used to tell were her actual adventures.

Finally the men stopped in front of a large imposing building which must be the palace. Guards with large spears stood on either side of an entranceway. The three men dismounted and the two knights handed the reins of the horses to Walter. They instructed Walter to stay there with the horses and the prisoner. Prisoner…they meant me!

Walter tied the horses to a rail and led me by the rope over to a well. He pulled a bucket of water up and drank from it. He looked at me thoughtfully and then with a gesture offered me the bucket. My throat was dry from all the dust kicked up by the horses so I took it and drank thirstily. The water was gritty and had a slightly unpleasant taste to it. But I was so thirsty I didn't care.

"Where are we Walter?" I asked. "Outside Jerusalem, the holy land you fool!" he snapped. "My name is Walter, squire to Sir Edward, a knight of St. John and one day I too shall be a knight of St. John. You don't call me Walter, you call me sir, peasant! Now be quiet before I slice off your nose for being insolent!" With that outburst our pleasant conversation ended.

We stood in silence for about another 20 minutes before Sir Edward returned from the palace. "Come boy," he said as he took the rope from Walter. "King Richard wants to see you. Now boy, the Lion Heart is a busy man so stand quietly until he asks you a question and then answer it honestly and he may allow you to keep your head."

Richard the Lion Heart, I've read about him in history lessons. He was the king of England, a fearless warrior with a fearsome temper.

Grandma's watch has got me into serious trouble.

King Richard the Lion Heart

by Richard Jones

We entered a spacious chamber with a marble floor and a large throne like chair. In front of the chair, on their knees were three knights. In front of them was a tall, powerful man with broad shoulders and red gold hair and predatory gray eyes. "You've lost another battle, how are you ever going to capture Jerusalem… Get out, get out before I take your titles, your lands and your heads!" boomed the tall man. He could only be King Richard and then he turned those scary gray eyes on me.

"Who is this foul smelling peasant?" snarled King Richard. "This is the strange boy I told you about," replied Sir Edward. "He doesn't look much like a spy, although he is dressed strangely," pondered King Richard. "Well who are you boy?" continued the King. "Well sir," I began, "My name is also Richard, Richard Jones. As strange as it may seem I'm from the future and I came here because of this watch," I said, reaching into my pocket. As I held the watch it started beeping. King Richard and Sir Edward quickly jumped back. "Sorcery!" cried King Richard. "What type of evil magic makes this infernal sound?" I pressed the little button that stopped the watches' alarm. "Guards seize him!" yelled King Richard and two men at arms roughly grabbed me by the arms sending the watch tumbling to the ground. "Take him to the dungeon!" demanded the king.

Frantically, I reached down and grabbed the watch that was lying on the ground beside me, just as the two guards dragged me from the room and down a passageway. They opened the stout wooden door and hauled me down a steep stairway. At the bottom was another passageway that ended with a black metal door. The guards opened the door to reveal a small chamber with burning torches and another guard with a set of keys hanging from his neck. "Here you go, lad. Tuck the jailer will find somewhere nice for you to stay," laughed one of the guards. Tuck opened the door with one of the keys revealing a dark and gloomy room with straw scattered across the floor. The two guards lifted me and threw me into the cell and the door slammed shut.

As I picked myself up from the floor, I sensed movement in the gloomy darkness of the room. I wasn't alone. I heard the clanking of chains as a figure rose from the gloom in front of me. I jerked back in fright and backed up against the wall of the cell. "No need to be afraid," croaked the figure in front of me, "It's only me Mad Malcolm."

Mad Malcolm was huge with a wild tangle of red hair and a matching beard. He had several teeth missing and a nose squashed across his face. His hands were in manacles drawn together by a chain. "What's your name, lad?" He asked this question rather politely which was a bit of a shock for he looked like a terrifying dungeon dweller. So I told him my name and how I was first accused of being a spy and then some kind of evil magician.

Malcolm told me his story of how King Richard had also had him thrown in the dungeon. Mad Malcolm's real name was Sir Malcolm Douglas, a knight from Scotland. The English and the Scots have had many wars against each other and even on a crusade to win back Jerusalem they still didn't get on very well. Malcolm had defeated King Richard in a practice fight and afterwards King Richard had made what Malcolm considered to be a rude remark about his beloved Scotland. He flattened King Richard with his wooden practice sword and as a result he was flung into jail.

How did I get myself into this situation? I should have listened to dad! I sat down and put my head between my hands and thought about my mom and my grandma. Was this the type of adventure that they wanted me to explore?

And then I heard a whimpering, it was soft and barely audible among the noises of the dungeon. "Is that you Mad Malcolm, are you okay," I asked. "No it's Mohammed, he cries day and night, but don't worry about him...he belongs to the other side." I moved towards him and could finally see him. He was only a young boy aged five or six. His eyes were huge and he put his hands out to fend me off. I told him that I was his friend and I would not hurt him. "Friend... won't hurt," he said in broken English. I put out my hand and he took it. Then he wriggled closer and cuddled up to me. "Home please," he begged.

He was asking the wrong person. I didn't even know where I was...let alone how to get out of here. "Where are your parents?" I asked. He told me that he didn't know where they were but that he lived in a small town outside the palace.

I told Mad Malcolm that I needed to escape and take the boy home. He laughed at me and called me a fool. "I've tried to escape from here and if I can't get out, you and your little friend here will never get out." Maybe I was a fool to think I could escape, after all I'm only a kid myself.

Eventually I drifted off to sleep with Mohammed cradled under my arm. Grandma came to me in my dreams. She told me to use the watch to escape and take Mohammed back home. "Think about what you did to get here in the first place," she said softly in my ear.

The next morning I awoke sore and stiff. The smell made me feel like throwing up, it was disgusting in there! The guards walked past and threw some dried up, mouldy hard bread at us. Mad Malcolm pounced upon it and pushed Mohammed away. "Please…" begged Mohammed. Mad Malcolm tore off a small piece of bread and gave it to Mohammed. He greedily shoved it in his mouth and almost swallowed it in one go. He was obviously starving to death, I had to do something.

When things had settled down and Mad Malcolm had gone to sleep again, I took Mohammed into the corner and whispered that it was time to escape. I pulled out the fob watch and put it between both of our hands. I told him to think of home. The watch started to give off heat, Mohammed looked at me with fear. And then the tumbling sensation happened again, but this time Mohammed was with me. We landed with a huge thump in the sand.

Several people were surrounding us and talking in a strange language that I had never heard. Then someone recognized Mohammed. It was his mother, she had tears pouring down her face as she grabbed and tightly held her dear son. She held him in the air and everyone rejoiced with happiness. It was then that the attention turned back to me. People were pointing and looking scared and they slowly started to move away from me. Mohammed looked at me with his big brown eyes and said thanks. His mother's smile was warm and happy. I had done my job there.

I held onto the watch, closed my eyes and thought of home. Once again the watch became hot and I could feel myself drifting into the tunnel and falling and falling until bang I landed on my bed. I opened my eyes and everything looked normal. But then I looked at my clothes, they were torn and dusty.

Dad had heard the bang when I landed back in my bed and he came in to check on me. He looked me up and down and then put his fingers over his nose. "Richard, you're filthy and you stink! Go and have a shower and put those disgusting clothes in the washer." He started to walk out and close the door then he stopped and looked back at me. "Your mom would be horrified at how dirty you are." He shook his head and walked out.

My mom would be proud of me. I know she would. But I can't tell dad about my adventure, he wouldn't believe me and he'd probably take the watch away from me. Mom said this has to be my secret. I bet mom and grandma both know what I did today.

Monday

Back to school today. It was a little boring after yesterday and I found it really difficult to concentrate. I kept thinking about Mohammed and wondering what he was doing today. Was he going to school, looking after goats or just playing with the other kids in his village? I feel really proud of myself, saving him from that dreadful dungeon and almost certain death from starvation or disease.

Then I started thinking about all the different places and times throughout the ages I could visit. The possibilities were endless!

Honestly, I don't think I heard one word any of my teachers said today.

After lunch we had assembly and something really great happened. We WON the poster competition! I get to go with Maddi and Gretel to the Waterpark on Saturday. I am so excited! I've never been to a waterpark and I've never been down a waterslide – ever. It is going to be so much fun, especially with Maddi…oh and Gretel too.

Wednesday

At lunchtime today Ted and I went to the sports field and joined in a soccer game. I don't usually go down there and play, but Ted asked me to go with him. It was just a casual game and I was really enjoying myself, it felt great to run and work-up a sweat. That was until some of the jocks arrived.

They stood on the sideline and started calling us names. I just ignored them and kept playing. But Ted got really angry. You see, they decided to call him Princess. "Get the ball Princess!" they called. "Hey Princess, you missed the goal!" And they kept on picking on him. Of course they could see that they were getting to him. The angrier he got…the more they called out. He managed to control himself, but then they called out to me, "Look, there is the poor little girl who lost her mother." I stopped and looked at them, my mouth wide open and lost for words.

Then like a bomb about to explode, Ted stopped dead still in the middle of the field. His face turned a crimson shade of purple and he started screaming and running towards them. At first, they just laughed. Then the laughing stopped and they turned and started running away from Ted like a farmer being chased by a bull. "Come back you bunch of cowards!" yelled Ted. But they kept on running.

Ted eventually gave up and came back to me. "You okay?" asked Ted. "Yeah, I'm fine, thanks Ted, you're a real friend," and I slapped him on the back. We went back to our soccer game. Everyone laughed at the "tough boys", the "cool kids", the "jocks" and how quickly they ran off. We all felt good about ourselves. Ted standing up to the bullies like that really made my day. We all made a pact that we would never let them call us names and bully us ever again.

Today Ted became a hero in our eyes. I'm sure he grew a couple of inches taller in those few minutes. Way to go Ted!

Saturday

Waterpark Day! It was the best day ever! The girls were a little scared to begin with and secretly so was I. The slides are so high! But of course I didn't show my fear, I wanted to impress them. We went on so many slides, up and down, up and down. Laughing all the way!

Then towards the end we saw one of the teachers. Maddi doesn't like him and she wanted to get away before he got up the stairs. She thought she would go down faster by using more mats. Good thought, but it didn't work. Some of the mats came apart and got stuck in the tube. When the teacher came down he got stuck! Maddi's extra mats had blocked the tube. We laughed so hard, we had tears coming down our faces.

But then all the workers started running towards the slide. They had a panicked look on their faces. We stopped laughing and watched. They unbolted part of the slide and let him out. He didn't look happy! We quickly ran off and exited the park.

Maddi didn't mean to block the tunnel, it was an accident and nobody was hurt. Thinking back, it was the perfect end to one of the best days of my life.

Monday

When I saw Maddi and Gretel at school today we all burst into laughter. It was our little secret, we decided to tell nobody about the teacher tunnel incident. A story like that would spread like wildfire across the school. We decided to code name it the TTI (short for teacher tunnel incident).

After lunch we were walking to the library and guess who was walking out. Yep! He stopped and looked at us. I'm sure I could hear my heart thumping. Then he smiled and kept walking. Phew! He didn't recognize us, or did he?

This afternoon I had to make a speech about how we can stop the oceans from becoming more polluted. I hate talking in front of other people. My hands started shaking as soon as I entered the classroom. I felt hot and my hands started to sweat. Sitting in my seat waiting for my turn, I felt like I was going to faint. I was certain that I couldn't remember one fact from my prepared talk. And then I heard my name being called. Oh NO!!!

I walked to the front of the class and looked at all those faces. They all had bored looks on their faces. Who can blame them, I was the 21st talk they had heard over the last two days. Nobody wants to listen, they are either freaking out about the fact they have to get up soon or relaxing and thinking about something pleasant because they have already had their turn.

I held up my palm cards, but my hands were shaking so much it was embarrassing. I put them on the table in front of me. My knees felt like they were about to buckle and it suddenly felt very hot in that room. I went to speak and nothing came out. I tried again and a squeak came out. I could hear all the cool girls sniggering. What am I, a mouse! My teacher told me to take a deep breath. I did and then looked up. Maddi was in the middle row, she smiled and held up a note with TTI on it. I smiled, she is so funny. And then my speech just rolled off my tongue. I didn't even think about it, it all came spilling out.

My teacher was very impressed. My classmates were shocked...normally my talks were painful to watch. And when I finished, everyone gave me a huge clap. I had done it.

Tuesday

After school today, Ted and I went for a ride through the bush on our bikes down to the river. We were skipping stones on the water when Ted told me he didn't like Maddi. I was shocked, who could possibly not like Maddi. She is so nice and funny and normal. "She thinks she is pretty special, she is totally up herself," he complained.

I stood up for her, telling Ted that I really liked Maddi. But he just shook his head and told me I was wrong. "She is just like all the cool girls Richard, she is a pain," he said. I told Ted that if he gave her a chance and got to know her, he would definitely like her.

Maybe Ted is jealous of my friendship with Maddi? Maybe he really likes her, but isn't game to admit it? Could it be that he also has a secret crush on Maddi? I don't really care if he doesn't like her. I think she is amazing.

***

Friday

I'm really quite glad I didn't get into a sporting team. Reject sport or history club is really quite interesting. Today we talked about the Ancient Romans and the city of Pompeii. Our history teacher showed us pictures of the city that were almost unbelievable. So many people were caught trying to escape from the lava and ash and you can still see the bodies frozen in time. It would have been so frightening. One day I definitely want to visit Pompeii and just hope that the volcano doesn't blow up while I'm there.

Saturday

Dad went into the office again this morning. I tried to clean up some of the mess in the house but it just seems like a waste of time. I cleaned up the same things last week and they are dirty again. Maybe I should just ignore the dirt and mess.

I decided to go for a ride on my bike, but couldn't figure out where to go to. Then I thought about riding past Maddi's house. Maybe she'll be home and she'll see me and decide to come for a ride too. Either that or she'll think I'm a stalker! She lives about 10 minutes ride from my place, so off I took.

I was casually cruising down her street, pretending I don't know where she lives, when I see a man walk to the car parked in her front yard. He is followed by the biggest dog or should I say horse-dog I've ever seen. I thought Maddi lives with her Mom. Maybe this is her Dad? And I think the dog is a great dane. I wanted to stay and watch, but it just felt too obvious. So I kept on riding past their house and around the corner. I got off my bike and hid it behind a tree. I had to solve the mystery of who was visiting Maddi and her Mom. I felt like a detective who was about to solve a mystery.

Getting down on all fours, I crawled behind the hedges on the footpath until I was in front of Maddi's house. Everyone had disappeared back inside. Her house looks different to mine. Lots of flowers in pots, a peace sign and colorful little flags draped across the front deck. The curtains in one of the rooms were tie-dyed. It looks a little like a hippy house.

Then I could hear Maddi's voice. "Tyson, Dad!" she yelled. So it was her Dad. And that was when the automatic sprinkler system came on. The water was smelly and it landed all over me. Maddi's Mom came out and turned it off because the car doors were still open. I froze so she wouldn't see me.

Then I noticed a green ant climbing up my leg and it disappeared as it made its way under my shorts. I told myself not to panic. Then another ant started to make its way up my leg, followed by another and another. I was lying next to a nest. I tried to shuffle away and then I felt the first bite. I gritted my teeth shut. It really hurt! And then another one bit me. The pain was searing through my leg, but I still managed to stay still and not yell. But then the unthinkable happened and they all started biting me at once.

I screamed, jumped up and ran down the street. Looking back I could see Maddi's Mom staring at me, a look of shock and concern on her face. "Green ant bite!" I called out to her, "it's okay." I rounded the corner, raced behind the tree and pulled my pants down. There were about 10 ants all feasting on me. I slapped them off and pulled my pants back on. The pain was excruciating! I couldn't sit on my bike because most of the bites were near my bottom. I limped home, pushing my bike. It took over an hour!

The bites were red and raised, they looked really angry. I put some stop itch cream on them and lay on my bed on my stomach.

When Dad came home he asked if I was okay. What could I say? No, I was attacked by green ants while I was spying on a girl I like! That's just way too embarrassing! Boy did I learn a lesson today. When you are spying on a girl, don't do it next to a green ant nest!

Sunday

Last night I was feeling really bored and lonely so I took the fob watch to bed with me. The history club talk on Pompeii had really interested me, so I decided to see if I could take a closer look.

It was easy, I just thought about Pompeii in AD 79 on the 24 August. I closed my eyes and focused on the location and date. Before long the watch started to heat up and shine. Then I started tumbling through the tunnel and whamo I landed in bale of hay behind a stable full of horses. I had done it again!

I brushed myself off and wandered into the marketplace. There were people selling everything from live ducks to slaves to fine silks. The noises and smells were overwhelming. Imagine horse dung mixed with spices and roasting meat.

Some Roman soldiers were marching through the square. They were carrying a litter with an important looking old man sitting on a chair. Suddenly they came to a halt and lowered the man. He had a heavy gold chain around his neck and was dressed in a perfectly white toga.

As he approached each market stall, the men and women bowed to him and gave him gold coins. He must have been an important government official or maybe even a tax collector.

It was then that the ground shifted. The stalls rattled and pots fell and shattered. But the people just ignored it. They were used to the rumblings, they didn't know the awful fate that awaited them when the volcano, Mt Vesuvius erupted. The volcano was stirring. This was an earthquake. They needed to escape now before it was too late.

I had to warn them and save as many people as possible. I ran to the official to tell him about the impending doom. The soldiers blocked my way with their spears and told me to go away.

I looked around and found a group of children playing by the well. Grabbing their hands I tried to pull them towards the shoreline where I could see boats that could be used to sail them to safety. One of the boys called out and his father ran at me. He shoved me as hard as he could and I fell backwards hitting a soldier. The soldier also fell backwards and he knocked over the important man in the white toga. It looked like a bad case of dominos! Then the unthinkable happened. The important old man fell into a pile of horse poo. Everyone stopped, there wasn't a sound to be heard. Then the official climbed to his feet, the horse poo dripping off his formerly white toga. Breaking the silence he yelled, "Seize him!"

The soldiers grabbed me and tied my hands behind my back. Now I really knew I was in trouble. I could not reach my fob watch! I had no way of getting out of here and I knew the volcano was close to erupting.

They threw me in a cell and left me. Not another cell!

The ground shook again and the chains holding the door closed rattled violently. I called out to the guard and he begrudgingly came over. "You have to let me out, the volcano is going to erupt and everyone in Pompeii will die!" I warned.

He looked at me with his mouth hanging wide open. "You speak the same language as me, where do you come from boy?" I wasn't going to tell him Harper Valley (not after the last time). So I told him I was from Britain. He started to tell me about how he had grown up in Britain and all about his family. He just didn't get the urgency, but then again, he didn't know what was about to happen.

"Mt Vesuvius is going to explode!" I yelled at him. He told me not to be silly, it was just the Gods moving their furniture, it happens all the time.

At that very moment…Mt Vesuvius decided to blow her top.

A tremendous boom almost deafened us. We were both

thrown off our feet. Villages and soldiers ran past in mass hysteria. Everyone was panicking! The guard stood up and turned to run. "Help me!" I screamed. He turned and quickly unlocked the door. Then he pulled out a long curved knife. He was going to kill me. I lowered my eyes and started to pray, then he spun me around and cut the ropes that had tied my wrists together. He slapped me over the head, smiled at me and ran for his life.

I looked towards the volcano. Smoke was streaming from the top and pieces of pumas were starting to fall on the village. Then the sky started to blacken. Day turned to night as hot burning dust began to cover everything.

In their panic to escape, the adults had left behind the young children who were playing by the well. The ones I had earlier tried to rescue. They huddled together, afraid and crying for someone to help. I ran to them and took their hands telling them to follow me to the seashore. A wooden sailing ship was about to depart. One at a time I threw the children into the arms of a sailor on board the ship, as it started to move away from the shore.

At least they would be safe. Around me there were hundreds of people who would have no boat to escape on. Many of them rushed back under cover. As I wander through the chaos, I see the government official is sitting on his litter chair, demanding that someone take him away. The soldiers and people ignore him.

As the sky grows even darker, I reach for my watch. I have done all I can here. It was time to go home.

Once again I land in my bed with a thump. And once again, Dad comes in. "Richard, you stink! Don't you ever shower!" yelled Dad.

That was a close call!

Monday

Maddi wasn't at school today. She has gone to Hawaii for a holiday. Apparently her Dad has moved back in and they have gone for a family get-together. I hope she has an awesome time. I'd love to go to Hawaii. I'll miss her.

***

Friday

This has been a very boring week. School's been boring. Home's been boring. Sorry diary, I've got nothing for you.

Monday

We had a maggot incident at school today. Unfortunately it involved Maddi. Our Deputy Principal (she is really nasty) called Maddi out of class today because she had maggots coming out of her bag. Poor Maddi! She must have left food in her bag before she went to Hawaii. I felt so sorry for her. Imagine being the new girl at school and having that happen to you. To make it even worse, Ted has started calling her maggot. He was so horrible during lunch break. Maddi was just trying to pretend like it didn't happen, but Ted wouldn't let it go. She looked at him with absolute loathing. I'm going to talk to Ted tomorrow and tell him to leave her alone.

I tried to talk to her, but she just blushed and kept walking. I wanted to tell her that we had maggots coming out of our rubbish bin in the kitchen last week. At first I thought it was spilled rice, until I saw one move. Yuck! Dad and I have decided to take the rubbish out every day from now on. I just wanted to let her know that these things happen to everyone and she shouldn't be so embarrassed. I'll just have a quiet word to Ted and get him to back off.

Today I got my mark for my talk on Ocean Pollution. I got an A! I can't believe it, I never get an A for a spoken presentation. I always get a C. To be honest, I didn't think it was possible for me to get higher than a C. Now that I have proved that theory wrong, I plan to get a B or an A next time as well. I just have to be more confident and less nervous.

We also did cooking today and we made muffins. My muffin was delicious. I'm going to make some for Dad on the weekend. I hope Maddi and Gretel had more success this time as well. Miss Moffat must have decided to stick clear of another possible raw meat disaster.

Tuesday

I talked to Ted today. Actually I asked him to lay off Maddi. He told me he just doesn't like her, but for me he will try to be nicer. However, I did hear him whisper "maggot" as he walked past her on the way to English.

***

Friday

Something horrible happened to Ted today during class. It was after lunch and he must have had some chocolate cake stashed away somewhere. He was eating it and smiling. Then this terrible look came onto his face. He started spitting and spluttering, the chocolate cake was flying everywhere. And then I saw the problem. There were maggots in the cake.

Twice in one week! What is going on? I felt like throwing up myself. And then I glanced over at Maddi, she had a very smug look on her face. Did she have something to do with the maggots in the chocolate cake? She looked at me and smiled. I mouthed to her, "Did you do this?" Maddi shrugged her shoulders and smiled again.

After school one of the cool girls called Ted – Maggot Mouth. So cruel, but I suppose he kind of asked for it after calling Maddi, Maggot, all week.

I asked Ted where he got the chocolate cake from and he said his Dad made it. But I don't believe that, he probably stole it from someone and had it stored away for too long. Maybe I'll make Ted some muffins on the weekend as well.

History club was interesting again today. The teacher showed us a video on World War 1. Some of the boys who went off to war weren't much older than me. How frightening it must have been for them! I'm definitely not going anywhere near my fob watch this weekend!

Saturday

Maddi's mom called me this morning and asked if I would like to come and watch Maddi's first soccer match. I wasn't sure what to say and then she said that Gretel was coming as well and it was a surprise, so I gladly accepted the invitation.

I met her family for the first time. Her Mom is pretty cool and really easy going. Her Dad is really enthusiastic and outgoing. He shook my hand and said that he had heard great things about me. Me! What had he heard? Mrs. Bull wanted to know all about my family. I told her about Dad. Then she asked about my Mom...so I told her. She gave me a big cuddle. I was a bit embarrassed, I mean...I'd only just met her. I know my Mom would really like Maddi's Mom. They are kind of similar, both warm and caring.

Maddi's Dad is a little embarrassing. Okay, he is very embarrassing. He is one of those really loud encouraging dads. I could see that Maddi wanted him to stop calling out advice and cheering her on. I could see her cringing. But at least he cares.

The most amazing thing happened on the field. It had nothing to do with her soccer skills. They were pretty bad. Actually they were really really bad. One of the girls on the other team fell over and put her hands to her neck. She was turning purple, then blue. Maddi ran over and grabbed her. Then she put her hand into the girl's mouth and pulled out her broken mouthguard. The girl was actually choking to death. Maddi saved her! What a hero! She is incredible!

I think I'm falling in love....

***

Find out what happens next in

Diary of Mr TDH

Book 2

True Love

Thank you for reading my book.

If you enjoyed it, I would be very grateful if you would leave a review on Amazon.

Your support really does make a difference!

Some other books you will love...

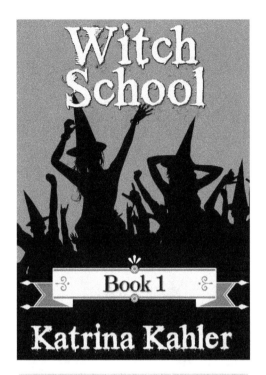

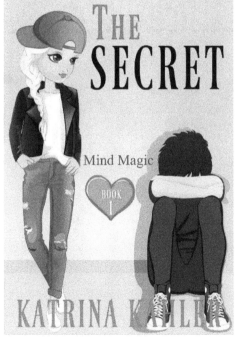

ZERO TO HERO

BOOK 1

BILL CAMPBELL

HOW TO MAKE FRIENDS AND BE POPULAR

GIRLS ONLY!

KATRINA KAHLER
KAZ CAMPBELL

CPSIA information can be obtained
at www.ICGtesting.com
Printed in the USA
BVHW040228111220
595469BV00030B/836